"Give me your hand."

She couldn't stop laughing at the sight of this rugged guy sporting blue nail polish. She took the bottle of nail polish remover from the cupboard along with several cotton balls.

She forced herself to look only at the nail she was working on and not his face. But with each swipe of the cotton ball, she grew more and more conscious of how nice his hands were.

Touching him stirred an unwelcome attraction. But she was impressed with his willingness to let the girls cover him in stickers and paint his fingernails. She wouldn't have expected that from a die-hard bachelor. Aware of the tension between them, Lainie cleared her throat and attempted light conversation. "My girls can be very persuasive."

"A couple of little charmers. They told me this color matched my eyes."

"Oh, no. Your eyes aren't sky blue, they're cobalt like those old bottles…" She froze. What was wrong with her?

"I'm partial to brown eyes myself."

She had brown eyes.

Lorraine Beatty was raised in Columbus, Ohio, but now calls Mississippi home. She and her husband, Joe, have two sons and five grandchildren. Lorraine started writing in junior high and is a member of RWA and ACFW and is a charter member and past president of Magnolia State Romance Writers. In her spare time she likes to work in her garden, travel and spend time with her family.

Books by Lorraine Beatty

Love Inspired

Home to Dover

Protecting the Widow's Heart
His Small-Town Family
Bachelor to the Rescue

Rekindled Romance
Restoring His Heart

Bachelor
to the Rescue

Lorraine Beatty

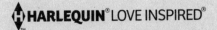

H **HARLEQUIN**® LOVE INSPIRED®
™

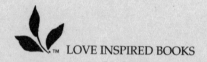

LOVE INSPIRED BOOKS

ISBN-13: 978-0-373-87959-5

Bachelor to the Rescue

www.Harlequin.com

Printed in U.S.A.

Search me, God, and know my heart;
test me and know my anxious thoughts.
—*Psalms* 139:23

To my sisters—Linda, Brenda, Tina and Kathy.
We may not be related by blood
but I love you all as if we were.

Chapter One

"Mommy, can we go home now? I'm tired of coloring."

Lainie Hollings fought back the nausea churning in her stomach and gently stroked her youngest daughter's hair. "Not yet, Chrissy. Why don't you use the green crayon for a while?"

A weary sigh accompanied the nodding of the little head. Lainie watched her girls, six-year-old Natalie and four-year-old Christiana, as they scribbled on the pages the officer at the Dover Mississippi Police Station had given them to keep them entertained. They couldn't go home because they had no home to go to. Her job as assistant to Mrs. Forsythe, a wealthy businesswoman in Memphis, Tennessee, had ended when her employer had moved away for health reasons. Thankfully, Lainie had quickly landed the position as head librarian for the Dover Public Library.

Today was their moving day. This morning, she had been filled with excitement and bursting with hope. This move marked the culmination of a dream she and her husband had once shared. They'd planned to leave Baton Rouge and its big city life behind and move to a small town where they could grow their family in a friendly, nurturing environment. They'd been saving for a house, but she had been forced to use the money for Craig's funeral instead. Alone and pregnant with their second child, she'd moved to Jackson, Tennessee to live with her mother and gone back to school at night to get her degree.

The past five years had been difficult, moving from place to place, job to job. The librarian position was her chance to find a permanent home.

So, they'd come to Dover a few days early to find a place to live and check into child care. It was supposed to be a fun trip discovering their new home. Instead, they were sitting in a police station, the victims of a crime. As they had been leaving a local restaurant, a man had shoved Lainie against her car, waved a gun in her face, then yanked her purse from her arm and fled. Thankfully, she'd already put the girls in the car. But all she had left were the car keys she held in her hand, and eight dollars and thirty-four cents—change from lunch, which she'd shoved into the pocket of her cotton slacks.

The moment replayed in her mind like a scene from a horror film, tightening the vise of fear around her chest. She lowered her head into her hands, fighting to keep the rising panic at bay. How was she going to take care of her girls? Where would they stay? She'd set aside money for a motel, but now, without a credit card or cash, that was impossible. Tears welled in her eyes and she brushed them away quickly, not wanting the children to see her upset. But she was barely holding it together.

"Look, Mommy, I colored it purple." Chrissy's blue eyes sparkled from behind her glasses.

"Good job, sweetie."

Looking at her precious girls, her throat constricted again. What if the thief had taken the car with the girls inside? What if he'd killed her? Lainie forced the terrifying thoughts aside. She couldn't give in to the fear. They were all fine, but destitute. She had no phone, no ID and no money. The only person she knew in town, Mr. Bill Ogden, mayor and president of the library board who'd hired her, was out of town for the weekend. They were on their own.

Unless Shaw McKinney showed up.

The knot in her chest grew. She clasped her hands together, squeezing tightly. While paying her bill at the restaurant, she'd noticed several business cards on display. One had a familiar name printed on it. Goudchaux McKinney Construction. Shaw McKinney, contractor. She'd picked up the card, the name unearthing anger and resentment she'd thought long buried. If it weren't for him, Craig would still be alive and her daughters would have a father. She'd shoved the card into her pocket along with the change. Shaw was the last person on earth she wanted to ask for help, but he was her only option. She'd given the card to the officer and asked him to call.

"Mommy, I have to go." Natalie wiggled in her chair.

Chrissy looked up, pushing her tiny glasses up on her little nose. "Me, too."

Lainie stood and looked around for her purse, wincing when she remembered it was gone. "Come on, girls."

Lainie took their hands and walked down the hall to the restrooms. She tried to quell the nervousness swirling in her stomach as she helped Chrissy wash her hands. Maybe when she returned to the lobby, Shaw would be here. She didn't want to think about what they would do if he didn't come. Worse yet, what if he did? Turning for help to the man responsible for her husband's death was repugnant.

Settling into the molded plastic chair again, she glanced toward the lobby entrance as yet another stranger walked in. She'd repeated this motion so often she now recognized the distinct squeak and swoosh of the door when it opened and closed. This time, it ushered in a gray-haired man carrying a large envelope.

"Mommy, can you draw me a rainbow?"

Lainie took one of the crayons and drew arched lines across the paper. "What's Shaw doing here in Dover, Mississippi, anyway?"

"What, Mommy?"

"Nothing, sweetie. I'm just talking to myself." The last time she'd seen Shaw was in Baton Rouge, Louisiana. Craig had hired on with Beaumont Construction, determined to learn carpentry so he could eventually start his own contracting firm. Shaw had been his instructor, the one assigned to show him the ropes and keep him safe as he navigated the dangers of the job. But he hadn't, and Craig had died.

Lainie pressed her lips together. They'd been sitting in the police station for two hours, filling out forms, answering questions. She had to face the possibility that Shaw might not come. He probably didn't remember her. She'd have to find another way to survive until she started her job next week. Maybe there was a homeless shelter in town. The idea made her sick. She'd worked hard the past five years to take care of her girls, and she'd done a decent job so far. But this wasn't the time to let pride stand in her way. Perhaps there was a church in town that could help. Their last resort would be to spend a few nights in the car until the mayor returned. Hopefully, he'd let her start work early or give her an advance to tide her over.

Closing her eyes, she clasped her hands in front of her mouth. *Lord, help me. I have no one. Nowhere to turn, but You. You've seen me through these past five years. Please don't abandon me now.*

Shaw McKinney ended the call and jammed his cell phone into his back pocket, grinding his teeth in exasperation. The drywall crew that was supposed to start today wasn't coming. Any more setbacks and this project might never be completed. He was already three weeks behind due to a series of unexpected delays. Thankfully, he'd obtained an extension, but the next deadline was set in concrete. Slowly, he walked through the old mansion. The 1885 house was one of the oldest in Dover and had been empty for the past dozen years. Thanks to an anonymous benefactor, the building, along with money for restoration, books and staff, had been donated to the town to replace the library, which had burned down five years ago.

Shaw had won the contract. It had meant not only a financial boon to his new construction business, but a huge boost to his reputation. After leaving LC Construction a year ago and starting his own company, McKinney Construction, he'd made the classic newbie mistake of overscheduling his projects. With the library job behind, he'd had to pull back on his other jobs because if this one wasn't done on time, he'd have to pay a hefty fine to the benefactor's foundation, one that could mean the end of his fledgling business. Shaw had factored in time for unexpected problems, but the old house had coughed up more than he'd bargained for.

"So, are they coming or not?"

"Not." Shaw faced his foreman and longtime mentor, Russ Franklin. The older man was the biggest asset to Shaw's start-up construction company. Skilled, experienced and dedicated, Russ had owned his own company in Alabama for years. When he had sold it, Shaw had convinced him to move to Dover to work with him. "Our drywall crew took another job. They couldn't wait on us any longer."

"That's going to put us further behind."

"How long would it take for you and me to do the work?" It was his last resort.

Russ frowned. "Too long. We're way too close to the deadline as it is. You want me to find us another crew?"

The knot in Shaw's chest, which had formed over the past few weeks, tightened. "Yeah. Call Laura Holbrook and see if she has a few guys we could use. Or maybe she knows of another contractor we can call. I've used up all my contacts."

Russ moved off to make the calls, and Shaw planted his hands on his tool belt and scanned the large room that would be the fiction section of the new Dover Library. It would take several days to put up drywall, then tape, float and sand before they could paint. Days lost when other crews couldn't work.

When Russ returned, his expression was grim.

"Laura doesn't have anyone to spare at the moment, and she doesn't know any other crews that are available."

Shaw rubbed his jaw. He couldn't handle another delay. Dover had been without a library for a long time, unable to afford a new one. The donation had been a blessing to the small town and generated huge excitement from the residents. The people here had given him a home and a fresh start. He wasn't about to let them down. Even if he had to work around the clock to get the job done.

His cell rang and he yanked it out of his pocket, frowning when he saw the name on the screen. Dover police. "Hello." He listened as the officer explained the situation. Shaw rubbed his forehead and nodded. "Yeah. I know her. I'll be right there." He hung up, his chest constricted so tightly he had trouble breathing. The last thing he needed was another complication in his life. And Lainie Hollings was a giant one.

Hearing her name had unleashed a landslide of painful memories and a heavy dose of guilt. He'd started to deny knowing her. It would do neither one of them any good to meet again. But when the officer had told him she'd been robbed, Shaw couldn't ignore her plight. Lainie was a widow because of his carelessness.

A death he could have prevented. He'd double- and triple-checked her husband's safety harness on the roof that day, only to find he'd loosened the straps again. Irritated with Hollings's cavalier attitude, Shaw had failed to check again, and Hollings had fallen from the roof. Lainie blamed him for her husband's death. Shaw accepted his part in the accident. He should have checked again. A dozen times if necessary. But he hadn't.

"Everything okay, boss?"

Shaw looked at his foreman. Right now, nothing was okay. "I've got to leave. I might not be back today. Keep looking for a crew and check on the remodel on Corey Road. If we can get that job done, we can list it."

Russ nodded. "And what about the Hanson remodel?"

Another problem to add to the pile. "I'll have to push them back again." Russ frowned and Shaw held up a hand to halt the comment he knew was coming. The Hansons were beyond irritated. If he didn't find a way to soothe their ruffled feathers, it could get ugly. But that was the least of his worries now.

Shaw climbed into his truck and cranked the engine, trying to figure out how he'd face Lainie Hollings. What did you say to the wife of the man you killed?

The moment he stepped inside the police station, his attention was drawn to the dark-haired woman seated in the waiting area. His stopped in his tracks, his heart racing, the blood roaring through his ears. She was even lovelier than she'd been when he'd first seen her. That moment was indelibly etched in his mind. She'd come to the job site to bring her husband his lunch. They'd laughed and talked and shared little touches, and Shaw's heart had grown envious.

Lainie had caught him watching her, and he'd felt a jolt like an electrical charge through his system. She was the prettiest woman he'd ever seen. She'd looked away and that's when the shame had tightened his throat. What was wrong with him? Admiring the wife of the man he was training was detestable. Shaw had gone back to work and vowed to keep his attraction in check.

Realizing he was still standing in the doorway, Shaw

squared his shoulders and stepped forward. Lainie was hunched in her seat watching two little girls as they scribbled on paper. Her dark brown hair was shorter now, falling in a sleek line to her shoulders. She glanced at him. In that moment, he noticed the sparkle was missing from her big brown eyes. Instead, he saw fear and anxiety. She looked fragile and alone. He was hit with a strong desire to pull her close and comfort her, but he didn't have the right. All he could do was offer his help. His attraction had no place in this situation.

The door to the police station swooshed open again, but Lainie didn't bother to look.

Shaw wasn't coming. She'd have to find help someplace else. Heavy footsteps on the floor drew her attention, and she looked up to see a tall, dark-haired man. He was dressed in faded jeans and a dark T-shirt with a company logo that hugged his torso in an interesting way. His sturdy, tan work boots thumped the floor as he strode toward them with a confident swagger. She started to look away only to realize who the man was. Shaw McKinney.

She didn't remember him looking like this. He was taller, more imposing than she remembered. His shoulders were wide enough to carry the world. Her inspection moved to his ruggedly handsome face. Navy blue eyes. Deep lines in his cheeks. His sharply angled jaw was softened by firm lips and a dimple in the center of his chin. A flicker of appreciation darted along her nerves, squelched instantly with humiliation. How Shaw McKinney looked had nothing to do with the kind of man he was. His actions had cost her everything.

His eyes bored into her as he came closer, and there

was a grim set to his jaw. Her hopes faded. He wasn't any happier to see her than she was to see him. She shouldn't have called him. Asking for his help was a betrayal of her husband's memory. Natalie looked up at her with a sweet little smile, reminding her that she had to think of the girls first. She forced the nausea aside and raised her chin, clasping her trembling hands in her lap.

"Lainie, are you all right?" He glanced at her then down at the girls, his forehead creasing in a deep frown.

Stupid question. No, she wasn't all right. She stood. "I'm fine. Thank you for coming. I'm sorry to bother you, but there was no one else to call."

"You did the right thing." He motioned her to be seated.

Shaw stared at the girls, a shadow seeming to pass behind his eyes. Was he feeling guilty? Good.

Her conscience pricked, but she ignored it, sinking into the chair as her knees began to fail.

Natalie had been two years old when Craig died. Chrissy not yet born. "Shaw, this is Natalie and Chrissy. Girls, this is Mr. McKinney. He—" What did she say? He's the reason you don't have a daddy? "Is someone we knew a long time ago."

Shaw sat, leaving an empty chair between them. "Tell me what happened. The officer who called said you'd been robbed."

She nodded. "We were leaving the restaurant and as I was getting into the car a man waved a gun at me, grabbed my purse and ran off. It all happened so fast I couldn't even react."

His gaze landed briefly on both the girls and he set his jaw. "How did you know I was here?"

Lainie set Chrissy on her lap, taking strength from

the little body. "I saw your business card at the diner. It had your partner's name on it so I wasn't certain it was you."

"Partner?"

"Yes. Someone named Gawdchalks?"

Shaw shook his head. "Goudchaux is my first name. It's pronounced God-shaw. My mother was Cajun French. When I started my business, I thought it sounded more professional, but all it did was confuse people so I went back to Shaw." He met her eyes. "I'm sorry this had to happen to you."

She ran her hand along Chrissy's ponytail. Tears welled behind her eyes, but she refused to let them fall in front of this man. "He took everything. My phone, my credit cards. Everything important was in my purse." She gulped in a breath of air. The thought of replacing all her information was overwhelming. "I have to close my accounts, contact my bank, but I don't have a phone, I don't know the numbers."

A warm hand rested upon hers, helping her focus and draining away the panic that was building in her chest. She took a deep breath, then remembered whose hand was touching her. She pulled away.

"It's okay. We'll get it all taken care of." Shaw rested his arms on his thighs. "What are you doing here in Dover?"

Lainie glanced away. It felt wrong confiding in him, telling him about her life. "I'm the new librarian. I'm supposed to start work this Thursday. We came to look for a place to live."

Shaw's eyes narrowed and a deep crease folded his forehead. He glanced around the room as a group of police officers strode through talking loudly. "Do you have a place to stay?"

"No. I was going to find a hotel after lunch."

Shaw touched his jaw. "The hotel has been closed for years. There are only two places here in Dover. The Dixiana Motor Lodge is nice, but they have very small rooms. I doubt the three of you would be comfortable. The Lady Banks Inn is a bed-and-breakfast, but it's pricey and filled with antiques."

Lainie sighed. Visions of trying to keep two energetic little girls from breaking a house full of priceless furniture and knickknacks made her head ache.

"Come on." Shaw stood. "You can stay at my place until you get things sorted out."

"Your place?" The thought sent a jolt of anxiety along her nerves. She was not going anywhere with this man. "Absolutely not."

Shaw's eyes darkened. "Then tell me what you want me to do. If it's money you need, tell me how much."

Embarrassment heated her cheeks. "No. That's not why I called you." Taking money from this man was out of the question. Not to mention demeaning. Clearly, she hadn't thought things through. How had this happened? Now she was committed to taking help from Shaw. She searched frantically for an alternative only to come to the realization there was no other choice. She and the girls would stay with him. She nodded, unable to find her voice.

"My truck is right outside."

She stood. "I'd better take my car. It'll be easier than trying to move the car seats. I can drive. The police gave me a temporary driver's license." She looked around on the nearby seats for her purse. Her heart sank. No purse.

No things. The shoulder on which she always draped her bulky purse felt empty. Shoving the coloring pages into her pocket, she took the girls' hands and started walking, acutely aware of Shaw right behind her.

The early June sun had sent the temperature into the midnineties, creating waves of heat that rose from the pavement in the parking lot. Lainie swallowed and wiped her brow. Shaw stood nearby as she helped the girls into the car and buckled them in. She stepped to the driver's door and reached for the handle. A wave of asphalt-heated air rose up and engulfed her, weakening her knees and causing her to sag against the side of the car.

Strong arms slipped around her waist, holding her upright. They turned her around and into a wall of warm strength and safety. No longer able to contain her emotions, she gave in to tears, sobbing against Shaw's chest. She wanted to stay here forever. It felt good to have someone to lean on. The weight of single parenthood grew heavy at times. But then, like a cold wave on the shore, reality crashed over her. She pushed back, horrified to see she'd clutched his shirt in her fist. She avoided his eyes. "Sorry." She reached for the car door, but Shaw stopped her before she could open it.

"You're in no condition to drive."

"I'm fine. I can take care of myself." She shot him a withering glance. "I've been doing it for a long time now." She sensed Shaw recoil.

"I'm well aware of that. But right now I'm taking care of things." He walked her around to the other side of the car and eased her inside. "Give me your keys."

"What about your truck?"

"I'll get it later."

Lainie leaned back in the passenger seat, too tired and weak to resist. She hated feeling helpless, but there was nothing she could do for the time being. Turning her head away from Shaw, she tried to ignore him. It wasn't easy. He took up a lot of space in her small car. She stole a quick glance as he adjusted the seat farther back to accommodate his long legs. He looked uncomfortable in her compact car, but she could easily see him in the cab of a sturdy pickup.

"Are we going home, Mommy?"

"No, Natalie. We're going to Mr. Shaw's house. It won't take long to get there."

Turning her attention to the window again, she allowed the sights outside to temporarily distract her. Dover was a charming town. With its courthouse park and streets lined with picturesque buildings, it was the kind of place she'd dreamed of raising her children. A community of love and support with friendly neighbors, and people who took care of one another. She was going to like it here once she got past the unpleasant welcome.

A few blocks beyond the square, Shaw turned onto a street in an older neighborhood. Large Victorian homes with manicured lawns and full-grown trees brought a small smile to Lainie's lips. She'd always had a fondness for gingerbread houses. To her, they represented home, family, permanence—all the things she wanted for her girls and never had herself.

Shaw slowed the car and pulled into a driveway. Lainie scanned the facade, disappointed at what she saw. Unlike the other lovely homes on the street, this house was in need of love and attention. The paint on the Queen Anne Victorian was faded. The turret rising up on the left side of the house was elegant, but the finial at the top was bent in half. The roof was missing several tiles. Many of the spindles on the front porch railing were gone.

Shaw shut off the engine and handed her back her keys. "It's not much, but it's home."

Home? The word sent a cold splash of reality over her nerves. She could *not* under any circumstances stay in this man's house. What had she been thinking? "Maybe you'd better take us back to town. Is there a homeless shelter here?"

Shaw shifted in his seat to look at her. "Do you really want to do that? This house is a duplex, Lainie. The former owner had divided it up years ago. You'll have your own space. The yard is fenced so it's safe for your kids. It's temporary. Until you can get your documents replaced. Please. I can't let you go to a shelter."

He was right. She was here for only a short while. Until she could replace her stolen bank cards. Then she could find a place to live. Faraway from Shaw and the past. In a way, this was all his fault. He owed her that much. And she was far too tired and upset to fight another battle right now.

Lainie reached for her purse. How many times would she do that before she remembered she didn't have it any longer? She climbed from the car, then opened the back door to help the girls. Natalie jumped out and stared at the house. Chrissy unfastened the buckles over her chest and joined her sister.

"Mommy, is this a castle?"

"No, just an old house." Aesthetically, the home was lovely. A stately two story, with wraparound porch and dripping with gingerbread. With some work, it could be the most beautiful home on the street.

She steered the girls to the front steps, noting the spacious porch was perfect for wicker furniture. Large ferns stood in corners. A weather-beaten swing hung at the far end, beckoning her to sit and relax.

Lainie followed Shaw into the spacious main hall, her gaze taking in the high ceilings and the stately staircase rising to the second floor. The inlaid wood floors were dark from years of neglect, making it hard to discern the pattern. The wide center hall stretched to the rear of the home. To the right were two large pocket doors partially open to reveal an empty room, probably the original parlor. On the other side of the entrance was a thick, unattractive door with a sturdy lock.

"I'll be right back." Shaw disappeared behind the staircase.

"I want to climb the stairs." Natalie pointed to the elegant stairway with stately newel posts and carved spindles below a wide smooth banister.

"Not right now, sweetie."

Lainie's gaze drifted from the exquisitely carved stairs on one side of the hall to the wall on the other. Two crudely constructed sections stood out like an ugly patch on a pretty face. She guessed the additions had something to do with covering up old doors and sealing off that side of the home. The house had an odd, schizophrenic feel to it. One side grand and stately, the other run-down and hopeless.

"Mommy are we going to live in this castle?"

"For a little bit. Mr. Shaw is going to help us until—" How did she explain to young children the predicament she was in without alarming them? And how did she keep her own fears under control? "Until I can get a new purse."

A loud bark shattered the silence. A black-and-white blur darted from behind the stairs and charged at them. Natalie screamed. Chrissy stood still, clenching her little hands into fists at her side. Lainie's heart pounded violently as a large dog barreled down on the children. She pulled her girls close shielding them with her arms.

"Beaux. Heel." Instantly, the Dalmatian slid to a halt, then trotted to Shaw's side.

Lainie glared at the man as he approached. Natalie pulled out of her arms. Lainie grabbed the back of her shirt to hold her back.

"I want to pet the doggie."

"Absolutely not."

"It's all right." Shaw commanded the dog to sit then stooped and gestured to the girls. "Want to meet my dog?" They nodded and took small steps forward. Shaw extended his palm. "Hold your hand like this and let him sniff you."

With the animal under control, Lainie relaxed her hold on her children. Both girls followed Shaw's instruction, giggling with delight when Beaux sniffed their fingers.

"Now pet his head and he'll be your friend forever."

Natalie scratched the dog's head and ears vigorously, while Chrissy moved to the dog's side and stroked his black-and-white fur. She smiled at her mother. "He has polka spots."

Lainie's heart still pounded, but at a more normal rate now that it looked as if the animal wasn't going to eat her children.

Shaw rose and joined her. "He's a very gentle animal, but rambunctious."

"You should have told me you had a dog."

"Would it have made a difference?"

"Yes." She crossed her arms and glared at him.

Shaw raised an eyebrow, challenging her statement.

Lainie turned away. She wasn't in a position to turn down his help. Dog. Horse. Dragon. It wouldn't have made a difference because she had nowhere else to go.

For the time being, she and her daughters were at the mercy of Shaw McKinney. It was Friday afternoon. It would be Monday before she could sort out her financial situation and meet with the mayor. Time in which she'd have to rely on Shaw. Not a comforting thought.

Chapter Two

"You'll be staying on this side of the house." Shaw unlocked the bulky door beside her, pushed it open, then handed her the key.

With a hand on each daughter's shoulder, she urged them into the large living room, pleasantly surprised at what she found. The apartment was fully furnished. Everything was covered with sheets, but she could make out a sofa and chairs, and various small tables. The rooms looked livable despite the accumulation of dust. A little elbow grease should fix that. It was definitely preferable to sleeping in the car.

"The woman who owned the house lived here until she was into her nineties. After she passed, her family removed the sentimental items and left the rest. You should have everything you need."

The house was the embodiment of Victorian style. The large windows, with intricate moldings, were covered with aged lace curtains, but still allowed in plenty of sunlight. French doors provided access to the front porch. Beside it, the curved walls of the tower added another element of charm to the room. It was a welcome change from the cramped apartment she'd shared with her mother, and the small garage apartment her former employer had provided. The girls ran to the tower, peeking out the long narrow windows.

Natalie smiled over her shoulder. "Mommy, this can be our Princess Club."

Shaw gave Lainie a puzzled look. "Princess Club?"

"It's a game the girls like to play. They find a cozy corner and pretend it's their special castle where they can play dress up and do crafts."

Chrissy pushed her glasses up, her expression serious. "It's only for girls."

Natalie ran back to Beaux and hugged his neck. "And cute dogs." Chrissy smiled and nodded in agreement.

Shaw ran a thumb along his jaw. "Uh, Beaux is a boy dog."

The girls looked at each other. Then Natalie whispered in her sister's ear, generating an enthusiastic nod that sent the little girl's ponytail waving. "Boy dogs are allowed. But not real boys."

Shaw led them to the rear of the apartment into a large kitchen. The once-white cabinets were yellow with age, the laminate countertops worn and scratched, but there was a cozy quality that appealed to Lainie. She could envision a large family gathered here for a hearty meal, discussing the day's events, and sharing laughter.

Shaw rested a hand on his hip, glancing around the kitchen. "Everything works. I keep it up in case I have to rent it out. I'd hoped to restore the place and get it on the market, but that's on hold now."

"You were going to sell it?" How could anyone not want to live in this lovely home? Even divided in half it was amazing.

"A single guy doesn't need a place like this."

"But you'll have a family someday."

He drew his eyebrows together in a frown, one corner of his mouth lifting in a sardonic smile. "Me? And give up my unencumbered bachelor life? Not in this century."

She should have known. His statement reinforced what her husband had always said about him. He was the stereotypical self-absorbed bachelor, a man who liked the ladies, but wanted no part of the responsibility that came with a real relationship.

Shaw pointed to the narrow staircase at the back. "There are two bedrooms and a full bath upstairs."

That's when she saw it. The door-sized opening in the wall between her kitchen and the main hallway. She could see straight through to Shaw's kitchen. Setting her jaw, she faced Shaw. "What is *that*? You said we'd have privacy and safety. Not with a giant hole in the wall we won't."

Shaw grimaced. "Yeah. Just some exploratory work. I'll take care of it."

"When?"

"Today."

It suddenly occurred to her that she and her girls would be alone with Shaw in this house. Concern skimmed along her nerves. She was accepting help from a stranger. All she knew for certain was that he had been irresponsible in looking out for her husband. "Do all the door have locks?"

His blue eyes bored into hers. "You're safe here. I won't let anything happen to you."

Lainie pulled her gaze away from Shaw's probing assessment as her girls ran past.

"Mommy, look at the trees." Natalie pressed her nose to the multipaned back door that led to a wide back porch and a large yard.

"Trees," Chrissy said in awe.

Natalie looked over her shoulder at Shaw. "Mister, is there a swing?"

Shaw frowned, glancing at Lainie with a puzzled expression. "No."

Natalie's lower lip poked out. "But I wanted there to be a swing."

Lainie peered out the window, at the tall leafy trees above full shrubs and a wide green lawn.

"Mom, can we play in the yard? Please?"

She couldn't blame the girls for wanting to run and play. They'd never had a yard. Apartment life was limiting for children. She'd dreamed of a place like this to raise her girls. Maybe after she'd worked a few years, she could afford to buy them a home of their own. Lainie took Natalie's hair in her hands gathering it at the back of the little neck before letting it go. "Not right now."

Shaw cleared his throat. "Uh, Lainie, we need to talk. Maybe the kids could play outside for a while? Beaux can go with them. He's a great guard dog."

The serious expression on Shaw's face started the anxiety in her stomach swirling again. She sent up a quick prayer. She couldn't take any more bad news. "Girls, you can play outside for a while. Mr. Shaw and I need to talk. Take Beaux with you."

With squeals of delight, Natalie and Chrissy rushed out the door. Lainie gathered what little strength she had left and looked at Shaw. "What is it?"

Shaw dragged a hand down the back of his neck. His

dark eyes were filled with confusion and concern. Finally, he smiled. "Come over to my kitchen. You can use my phone and computer to get your accounts closed."

He'd changed the subject. Why? But he was right. First things first. She couldn't afford to have that crook charging her cards to the limit.

Shaw gave her an encouraging smile. "Don't worry. It'll all work out."

Oh, but she did worry. She had mountains of things to worry about, and relying on Shaw was at the top of the list. How could she depend on someone who couldn't take care of the people entrusted to him? Lainie followed Shaw through the opening. The minute her accounts were taken care of, she and her girls were out of here. She just had to hang on and get through the next few days. Once she started work at the library, everything would be fine.

Shaw settled Lainie at his kitchen table with his laptop and helped her get started on contacting her creditors to close her accounts, then he went outside to bring in her luggage. Having Lainie in his home created an odd tension in his chest and triggered a variety of unwelcome emotions. He'd never expected to see her again, let alone assume responsibility for her and her children. He'd worked hard to conquer the guilt associated with Craig's accident. But now, every time he saw Lainie and those girls, he'd be faced with the consequences of his actions. In less than an hour, his old doubts and remorse had clawed their way to the forefront of his mind.

He sent up a prayer for strength. Somehow he had to take care of Lainie and her children, and keep the past at bay, because he needed all his focus on the job. Too much was at stake.

After hauling in several suitcases and bags from Lainie's car, there was nothing else to distract him from the real problem—telling Lainie that her job wasn't going to start this week. Or the week after. While the residents of Dover were grateful for the donation made by the anonymous benefactor, the many strings attached had caused problems. One of the biggest was the rumor that beloved former head librarian, Millie Tedrow, wasn't going to return. Shaw wasn't sure how the townspeople would react when they learned Lainie got the job instead. He had to prepare her for what she might be facing, and it would be up to him to stand between her and the town. If she'd accept his help.

Lainie was still sitting at the computer when he returned. She shifted in her chair and her thick, dark hair brushed across her shoulders like a curtain of brown silk. She wore ankle-length sand-colored pants and a bright yellow top that skimmed her curves. He shut down his observation.

He hated to interrupt, but she needed to know the situation. She glanced at him and he looked into her warm chocolate eyes, feeling momentarily disoriented. He didn't remember her lashes being so long or her eyes so expressive. He could read her every emotion, and right now he read fear and anxiety. She was waiting for the next shoe to drop, and he was about to drop a big one. "How's it going?"

She nodded, chewing on her thumbnail. "Almost done."

She tapped a few more keys, her intense concentration evident in the rigid lift to her shoulders. He stepped to the back door, watching her little girls play. They resembled their father with their blond hair and blue eyes. Shaw rubbed his forehead. Funny, he only remembered one child.

"All done." Lainie came to his side, looking out at her daughters. "They needed to run and play. It's been a long day for them."

The weary tone in her voice concerned him. "You, too." She shrugged without looking at him. "Lainie, I need to tell you something about your job at the library."

"What?"

The fear that flashed through her eyes filled him with dread. Best get this over with. "You won't be starting work at the library this week."

"You're wrong. Mr. Ogden said I would start on the eighth. That's this Thursday."

"The library isn't finished." The confusion in her eyes made him want to hold her close, the way he had outside the police station when she'd nearly collapsed. His nerves still vibrated from holding her in his arms, inhaling the strawberry scent of her hair, feeling her tremble against this chest.

"What do you mean it's not finished? I don't understand."

"The project is three weeks behind."

"Project? I thought this was a new building."

Shaw dragged a hand across his jaw. "The old Webster House was donated to the city for use as the library, along with the funds to remodel it, and provide books and staff."

She crossed her arms, and frowned. "What happened? Why isn't it ready?"

"We ran into unforeseen problems. It happens. Especially in old buildings like this one."

Her eyes narrowed. "What do you have to do with it?"

"I'm the contractor."

Lainie's eyes widened in shock. "Why are you so far behind? Why didn't you stay on top of things?"

Her words scraped like a steel rasp across his old guilt. She had every reason to think he was at fault. "There were foundation problems, and we uncovered asbestos in the walls, then—"

She held up her hand to stop his explanation, then rested her fists on the sides of her neck as if protecting herself from more bad news. His heart ached. She looked so defeated. She'd been through so much and he was piling on more.

"Why didn't Mr. Ogden let me know?"

"I don't know. I'm only involved with the construction phase."

Shaw saw the full realization sink in. Her shoulders slumped and she leaned against the wall. "What am I going to do? I have to have a job."

He stepped closer, catching a whiff of her strawberry scent. "Don't worry. I'll take care of everything. It's the least I can do."

A flash of anger sparked in her brown eyes. "Because you owe me?"

He winced at the truth of her comment. "Yes. But I also want to help. None of this is your fault."

"No, it's not."

Shaw clenched his jaw. Her inference was clear. It was his fault she was a single mother. "But I can take care of things until you're squared away."

"Like that?" She pointed to the opening in the wall.

He grimaced. He should have thought about the opening. But then he hadn't been expecting his past to slap him in the face. "I'll fix it right now."

She leveled her gaze at him, then walked through the opening to her side of the house. With her back straight and head high, her posture told him he'd better fix it. If he wasn't so tied in knots, he would have found her attitude amusing.

In his garage workshop, Shaw inspected the extra lumber and other leftover materials he kept at the back. He moved a few pieces of scrap wood aside and picked up the single French door and leaned it against the work-bench. It wasn't the best solution to the hole in the wall, but it would have to do. His gaze fell on the coil of rope at the end of the counter. It would be the perfect size and length for a swing. He dismissed the idea. Lainie and her kids would be here for only a couple of days. Once she had her business settled, she'd be gone.

He hooked his tape measure onto his belt, shoved a few shims and screws into his pocket, then picked up the door and headed to the house. In the hallway, he rested the door against the wall, took some measure-ments, mentally calculating the best way to secure the door in the opening. Giggles and footsteps sounded overhead. Lainie's girls.

They were two little cuties, for sure. Natalie, with her long curly hair and deep dimples was full of spar-kle. She smiled and bounced every moment as if happy with life. The little one was more serious, with straight hair pulled back into a ponytail and wispy strands fall-ing around her face. Tiny glasses perched on a button nose added cuteness to her already-sweet face. It must have been hard raising them alone. How had they managed these past five years? Who had Lainie turned to for help? Family? Friends?

He'd tried to offer his help right after the accident, but she'd refused his calls, and at the funeral, she'd ordered him to leave, making it clear she blamed him for her husband's death. He could still feel the hot sting of her last words to him that day. "I don't need anything from you. Ever." But now she did, and he wasn't going to let them down. He'd protect them and provide for them until they were safe and settled. As long as they were under his roof, he'd make sure they had everything they needed. They were his responsibility now.

Shaw channeled all his energy into securing the door into the opening. He was stooped down, driving in the last screw when Lainie appeared on the other side of the door. She glared through the pane, a deep frown on her face. He knew what was coming.

"It's glass."

Her words were muffled. He nodded and shrugged. She pursed her lips and pivoted on her heel. A few seconds later, she pushed through his back door and stopped at his side.

"You can see through it. Don't you have some wood or something to cover this opening?"

"Not here at the house. I'm sure you can find something to hang over the door to maintain your privacy." He pushed to his feet. "I'm hardly ever here. You'll have the place to yourself most of the time."

A knock at the back door drew his attention. Russ stepped into the hall, glancing between Shaw and Lainie. "You still need that ride?"

"I'll be ready in a minute. Lainie, this is my foreman,

Russ Franklin. Russ, this is Lainie Hollings." Shaw ignored the stunned look on his friend's face. "I asked him to stop by and take me to pick up my truck. Is there anything you need me to get for you while I'm out?"

Lainie crossed her arms over her chest, her reluctance to ask for more help evident in her pursed lips. "Food. The girls will be getting hungry and all I have are a few snacks."

Shaw nodded. "No problem. Make me a list." After muttering a pleasantry to Russ, Lainie returned to her side of the house. Shaw looked at Russ and saw his dark eyes brimming with questions.

"So that's the woman whose husband fell."

Shaw set his jaw. He didn't want to discuss that day. "Yes."

Russ whistled softly. "Interesting how the Lord works things out."

"What are you talking about?"

"Putting this woman in your path again. Maybe He's telling you it's time to face a few things."

Beaux slipped in through the doggie door and trotted to Russ's side, wagging his tail at the rigorous rubbing he received.

Shaw ignored the comment and gathered up his tools. Russ was the only one who knew how the weight of Hollings's death had affected Shaw. The guilt over the accident had sent him into a dark place. He'd left Beaumont Construction and moved to Gulf Shores, Alabama, and hired on with Russ's company. When his behavior had started to affect his work, Russ had taken him under his wing, got him into church and helped him get his life back on track. Shaw had focused all his energy on mastering his craft, which had led to a job with Laura Durrant in Dover, a well-respected restorationist.

Russ examined the French door opening in the wall. "You used that to fill the hole?"

"Don't have anything else. The boys used all my plywood during class last week." He taught woodworking to some of the teens in town. Last week, they'd used the last of his plywood to make shelves for the church storage closet. He hadn't had time to buy more.

Inside the cab of Russ's truck, Shaw fastened his seat belt and stared straight ahead. "I had to tell her the library is behind schedule."

"What for?"

He glanced at Russ. "Because *she's* the new librarian."

Russ exhaled a long slow whistle. "Not Miss Millie, huh?"

"Nope."

"That's not going to set well with some folks."

"No kidding. I didn't live here during her time, but even *I* know that Millie is the only person the town will accept to run the library." Awarding the job to a stranger would cause a lot of hurt feelings and angry complaints.

"How'd she take it?"

"Not well. She's depending on that job to support her kids."

"That's a shame."

"Yeah. Another reason for her to hate me."

"You sure having this woman stay with you is a good idea? I remember how you were after the accident. I'd hate to see you backslide after all this time."

His friend meant well, but he didn't understand. "I can't turn her away. I owe her."

"So you're looking at this as some kind of atonement? It was an accident."

"Was it?" Shaw faced the side window. Was it an accident, or had he been negligent? Only the Lord knew for sure. He had relived the events leading up to that moment a thousand times, but had never found an answer that satisfied him. He doubted he ever would.

Lainie tucked the covers around her girls then bent to kiss them good-night. They looked so small in the big iron bed. They were her whole life and the reason she'd gone back to school to get her degree in library science. More than anything, she wanted to give them a real home, a place with roots and tradition. Because of her father's job, Lainie had grown up moving from one place to another, always the new kid with few friends and fewer ties. She wanted better for her girls, and Dover was the perfect place. Or so she'd believed until today.

"Mommy, I want to live in this castle forever." Chrissy held up her glasses and Lainie laid them on the nightstand.

Natalie rolled her eyes. "It's not a castle, silly. It's only a house. We're staying for a few days, then we'll find us a house of our own." She smoothed back Natalie's hair, her heart swelling with love.

"But I like this house." Natalie rolled onto her side. "Will our next house have trees in the yard?"

Chrissy sat up. "Can we get a dog? With polka spots like Beaux?"

"Polka *dots*. We'll see." Lainie gently pressed her youngest down into the covers. "Now go to sleep."

Lainie laid the girls' clothes on the window seat, taking a quick glance into the darkness. The moon was full, casting a stream of light across the wide yard and making the leaves sparkle. She had to agree with her girls. She liked the house, too. The window seat was cozy and inviting. She could imagine her daughters cuddled up reading or watching the rain. Despite its quirky appearance, there was a homey feel to the house. Too bad it belonged to Shaw McKinney.

Downstairs, Lainie set about cleaning up the kitchen, her emotions playing tug-of-war between gratitude to Shaw for a place to stay and irritation that she was indebted to the man who'd made her a widow. She tried to ignore the twinge of remorse that rose up. Shaw had done all he could to make them comfortable, including closing the hole in the wall to ensure their privacy. Though she'd had to tack an old curtain she'd found in the closet over the glass panes.

He'd thought of everything. Too bad he hadn't done that five years ago.

The silence in the old house suddenly pressed in on her, unleashing the loneliness that always lurked in the recesses of her mind. She'd been a widow longer than she'd been a wife. She'd done the best she could the past five years, and the Lord had taken care of her and her sweet babies. He'd provided a home with her mother, then a home and a job with Mrs. Forsythe after Lainie's mom had died. But there were times she ached for someone special in her life, someone to lift the load for a moment or two.

She'd known that feeling for a brief second today when Shaw had kept her from falling. Until she had remembered who was holding her and what he'd done. Determined to overcome her depressing thoughts, she walked into the living room and picked up the toys scattered in the rounded corner, which was now the new Princess Club. As she passed the sofa, she noticed the cell phone Shaw had bought for her resting on the end table.

As much as she hated to admit it, Shaw was not what she'd expected. Craig had complained that Shaw was an arrogant bully, who strutted around the job as if he was better than everyone else. But that wasn't what she'd seen today. He'd returned from picking up his truck with enough food for a week and a cell phone for her. He'd convinced her to take it by pointing out she might need to call for help if he wasn't around. He'd even programmed in his cell number along with other local emergency numbers she might need.

His thoughtfulness irked her no end. It was obviously being driven by guilt. Well, she had news for him. Offering a helping hand now wouldn't erase his carelessness in the past. He might not be as arrogant as Craig had claimed, but that didn't wipe out what had happened.

Her thumb slid over the small phone screen. Still, it felt good to have a connection to the world again. She didn't feel quite so alone and cut off.

A gardenia-scented breeze stirred the aged curtains on the windows, beckoning her outside to enjoy the evening air. After the day she'd had, she could use a heavy dose of peace and quiet.

Stepping out onto the wide curved porch, she inhaled the heady fragrance of the elegant white blooms glowing in the moonlight. Lainie gripped the railing, allowing the sweet scent to soothe her frayed nerves and provide a new perspective on her situation. The day could have ended much differently. But the Lord had spared their lives, provided a place to stay and the means to restore her important information. The only glitch was the person sent to help them was Shaw—and the news her job wasn't going to start as planned. There had to be a mistake or an alternative.

She wanted to trust in whatever plan the Lord was working, but she couldn't see any reason for Shaw being the one to come to their rescue. Everything had been going so well, on time and on schedule. Now her life had been tossed in the air like confetti, the pieces scattered in all directions.

Turning toward the far end of the porch, she gasped when she saw a figure seated on the front steps. Shaw. He was stretched out along the top step, his back against the post, one knee bent and his arm resting on his leg.

"Why are you lurking there?"

"I'm not. You looked like you wanted some alone time. I didn't want to disturb you."

"You should have spoken up when I came out then I could have—"

"Run back inside?"

She opened her mouth to deny it, then changed her mind. She didn't want to give him the satisfaction of thinking he had any influence over her. Shaw stood and ambled toward her, his boots thudding with solid force on the old boards. He was a hard man to ignore. At five feet six, she wasn't considered petite, yet Shaw's height and solid mass made her feel dainty. Irritated by her wayward observations, she crossed her arms over her chest and raised her chin. He stopped a few feet away, but still close enough she could catch a whiff of sawdust. She'd always liked that smell. Quickly, she looked down at the cell phone in her hand.

"If you need to call someone, I'll leave you alone."

She shrugged, loneliness washing through her once more. "No one to call."

"No friends or family?" His voice was low and gentle as he studied her.

"Nope. Just me and the girls."

"I assumed when you left Baton Rouge you went back to your family."

"I did. I went to live with my mother in Jackson, Tennessee. Chrissy was born there. After Mom passed, I went to work for her good friend, Mrs. Forsythe, in Memphis. Now I'm here."

"I spoke to Mary Ogden this evening. The mayor's wife. She told me he'll be home around lunchtime on Monday. She said you should go by his office and speak to him about your job. She feels certain he'll do what he can."

She couldn't see his eyes in the dim light, but she didn't miss the conciliatory tone in his voice. He was still trying to make up in some way for the past. Something he could never do. "Can he get the library done by Thursday?" Shaw glanced away briefly, clearly stung by her question. She snuffed out the twinge of regret that surfaced.

"No. That's all on me, but I promise I'll get it done as quickly as possible. You can count on me."

She started to remind him that she'd counted on him to keep her husband safe. But as distasteful as it was to rely on Shaw's help, she couldn't ignore the truth. If it weren't for him, she and the girls might have been spending the next few days in a shelter, or living out of her car. He was doing all he could to help, even if his motivation stemmed from his own guilty conscience. She looked up at him and her gaze locked with his. The light had shifted and she could see the distress in his eyes. "I appreciate your help today. I don't know what I would have done otherwise. I'd do anything for my girls."

"Including taking help from me?"

Lainie squared her shoulders. "Yes." The flash of pain that shot through his eyes surprised her.

She opened the door and stepped into her living room. Shutting the door, she inhaled a few deep breaths to ease the anxiety clogging her throat. For the time being, she had no choice but to accept help from Shaw. But as soon as she met with the mayor, she'd convince him to let her start work whether the library was done or not. And the moment she received her new cards, she would find a place for her family to live and put as much distance as possible between herself and Shaw.

But as she lay in bed that night, one image kept reappearing in her mind. The flash of deep pain that had filled Shaw's eyes. Could the accident have affected him more than she'd thought? The notion disturbed her. If that were true, then her long-held assumptions about Shaw were wrong. And they couldn't be wrong. She'd placed him in a nice little box. Labeled neatly and precisely. Irresponsible. Not to be trusted. Her world was neat and orderly, and if Shaw wasn't the man she'd thought he was then that meant changing, and she didn't like change.

Besides, his whole nice-guy routine was an act calculated to ease his guilt and redeem himself for the past. Well, she had news for him. No amount of help or phony concern could make up for his careless disregard for others.

Chapter Three

Shaw pressed the trigger on the nail gun, the kick-back reverberating along his arm. The activity helped ease the knot in his chest, which had formed last night when Lainie had stepped onto the porch and stirred his emotions. Her presence was shattering the peaceful life he'd found and unearthing a past he'd fought hard to overcome.

Her thank-you had been frosty, but sincere nonetheless. Truthfully, he couldn't blame her. He'd feel the same way if he were in her position.

A few more pops and the half-round molding was secured. He picked up the next section and placed it against the paneling, making sure the mitered corners fit snugly. This room was one of two with paneled walls that needed major restoration. He was anxious to complete replacing the wainscoting and trim boxes. Then he could let the painters match the new stain to the old, and he and Russ could get started putting up drywall on the second floor.

The back of his neck tingled and he glanced over

his shoulder to see Russ eyeing him curiously. "You need something?"

"Nope. Just wondering why you're here so early on a Saturday?"

"We're behind. There's a lot of work to do."

"So it doesn't have anything to do with your guests?"

"Why should it?"

"I thought maybe you were anxious to get out of the house. The lady isn't happy to be staying with you."

That was putting it mildly. "Can you blame her?"

"Maybe not. But you need to stop blaming yourself." Russ strolled away.

Shaw pulled the trigger on the nail gun. Russ was never one for expounding on things. He stated his position and moved on, and he was probably right. Shaw should have paid for rooms at the Dixiana motel and gone on about his business. But he couldn't. Lainie might never forgive him for the past, but he'd do all he could to make sure she and her daughters were taken care of until the library was done.

Job complete, Shaw shut off the compressor, questions from the past surfacing again as he headed out to his truck. Had he done all he could that day? Or had he shirked his duty because of petty resentments? He'd been a different man then. Not nearly as safety conscious as he was now, or as experienced in dealing with a crew. Over the years, he'd learned how to spot troublemakers, slackers and guys who thought swinging a hammer was a thrill. If he'd known then what he knew now, he'd never have agreed to train Hollings.

What would Lainie say if he told her the whole truth about her husband? Would she forgive him then? Doubt-

ful. The truth would only tarnish her memory of him
and make Shaw feel like a heel.

He wanted to make things right somehow. Last night,
she'd stepped onto the porch into the moonlight and stolen the breath from his lungs. She was lovely, the kind of
woman he'd always hoped to find. The one he could spend
his life with. But she wasn't for him and never would be.

Shaw tossed his hard hat into the truck bed then spread
the blueprints on the tailgate. He flipped to the pages
showing the lobby layout. He tried to focus on the lines
and figures but found Lainie invading his thoughts again.

"Do all the doors have locks?" The panic in her eyes
had wounded him. Did she distrust him that much? Or
was she feeling vulnerable and scared in the aftermath
of being robbed?

She was in a tough spot and he wasn't sure how to
help her. Technically, she wasn't his problem. But how
could he stand by and let her and her girls struggle? He
was morally obligated to do whatever he could.

He stared at the blueprints, the web of tiny lines reminding him of his priorities. He needed to stop worrying about Lainie. His future depended on getting this
library finished. If the building wasn't completed, then
their personal problems were immaterial.

A silver truck pulled to a stop near his and his cabi-
netmaker, Jeb West, got out. They'd run into a glitch and
needed to find a way to reconfigure the reception desk.

Jeb hooked his hard hat under his arm as he joined
Shaw. "Hey, boss. I have a few ideas on how to rework
that counter."

"Good. I don't need any more complications."

Jeb lowered his head a bit and peered over his
glasses. "You okay? You're looking a bit sour."

Shaw frowned and grabbed up the blueprints. "You'd be sour, too, if you were weeks behind on a project." And your biggest mistake was living in your house.

"Hey, is it true Miss Millie isn't going to be the new librarian?"

"That's right." Word traveled faster than high-speed internet in Dover.

"Man, that's hard to believe."

The comment set Shaw's teeth on edge. "Believe it. People will just have to get over it. Lainie is going to be a great librarian. They need to stop being so bull-headed and give her a chance."

"Whoa. Don't bite my head off. I'd just as soon have a new librarian. Millie was a scary old—" Jeb cleared his throat. "Me, I'm all in favor of the new gal. I hear she's quite a looker, too."

Shaw let his anger fade. He was being overly sensitive. He needed to remember that not everyone was opposed to Lainie. Just a few old-timers who thought they were protecting their friend. One of those rumors, however, was absolutely true. "I think there will be a lot of folks who'll come to the library just to catch a glimpse of her."

Jeb stepped back to his truck and returned quickly with a blue-and-white striped box. Shaw chuckled. "The Donut Palace. Sugar covered?"

"I figured if you were here this early you might be in a bad mood. I was being prepared."

Shaw placed a friendly slap on his shoulder. "Let's get to work. After a doughnut break."

Lainie poured a second cup of coffee and carried it into the living room, stopping at one of the large windows facing the front porch. It was a beautiful morn-

ing. She would like to sit outside, but the swing was on
Shaw's side of the porch and she didn't want to cross
that barrier. Besides, if she sat outside, she might not
hear the girls, and she didn't want them alone when they
woke up in a strange house.

She hadn't slept well. Her dreams had been dark and
threatening, each one jolting her awake and making it
hard to fall back to sleep. In one, she'd been standing in
a lovely garden that had suddenly changed into a dark
cemetery. Another time, she'd dreamed she was running
down wet streets searching for something, but no idea
what. However, one dream had been more disturbing
than the others. She'd dreamed she was being carried in
strong arms against a solid chest and cradled in safety and
warmth. When she'd looked up, she had seen Shaw's face.
That nightmare had pulled her from sleep with a yelp.

Clearly, her subconscious was struggling to sort out
the events from yesterday. Back in the kitchen, she sat
at the table and opened her Bible, flipping through the
psalms. Like David, she was wandering in an unknown
wilderness, unsure of her direction and wondering what
the Lord was working in her life by putting Shaw in her
path again. She hoped his statement that she couldn't
start work on time was wrong. She planned on being
in the mayor's office the moment Mr. Ogden returned
to get things straightened out.

God willing, her replacement cards would arrive
quickly, and she could regain control of her life. She
glanced at the small makeup bag lying in the middle
of the table. She'd emptied it out to use as her temporary purse. In addition to the cell phone, Shaw had
given her a prepaid credit card for emergencies. She now
possessed the things she needed to function on a daily

basis—a temporary driver's license, a phone, a credit card and her change from the diner. It wasn't much, but it restored the sense of normalcy and control she'd been missing since being robbed yesterday.

"Mommy, I'm hungry."

Natalie shuffled to her side rubbing sleepy eyes. Lainie lifted her onto her lap. She was getting so big. "Did you sleep well?"

"It's a happy room."

"It is? Why do you say that?"

"'Cause the sunshine woke me up."

Little footsteps on the stairs announced Chrissy's arrival. She hurried toward her mother for a morning hug. Lainie's heart swelled with love and gratitude again for being delivered safely from a dangerous situation. She had her girls. Everything else could be handled in time.

Lainie prepared breakfast, enjoying the meal with new appreciation. Despite her feelings about Shaw, she had to admit she felt safe in this old house, and having a man nearby was comforting, too.

Chrissy swallowed the last of her juice then scooted off her chair. "I want to see Misser Shaw and play with Beaux."

Lainie had heard Shaw's truck pull out of the drive early this morning and assumed he was going to the library to work. "He's not here, sweetie."

Chrissy pulled back the curtain covering the French door. "Mommy, there's a note."

She joined her daughter, bending down to read the note taped to one of the glass panes from Shaw's side.

Working today. Call if you need me. Doggie door unlatched if Beaux wants to play.

"What's it say, Mommy?"

Beaux came to the door and sat down. Chrissy pressed her face to the glass and giggled. "Hi, Beaux. Do you want to play with us?"

Lainie ruffled Chrissy's hair. "Mr. Shaw is at work, but he said Beaux can play with you if you want."

Both girls squealed, threatening to burst her eardrums. They dashed out the back door and Beaux slid through the pet door to join them. Pouring another cup of coffee, she went onto the back porch to watch the girls play.

For a few moments, she allowed herself to daydream. If this were her yard, she'd clear out the bushes along the garage and put in a vegetable garden. And she'd put a small playhouse under that large live oak tree in the back corner. A sturdy one that would last until her grandchildren could play in it, too.

"Hello. Yoo-hoo. Over here."

Lainie looked in the direction of the shout and saw a woman about her age standing at the picket fence waving. Lainie waved back. "Hi."

"I'm Gwen Rogers. I heard the kids playing and thought I'd introduce myself."

Lainie joined the woman at the fence. Her smile was warm and friendly, making her blue eyes sparkle. "I'm Lainie Hollings."

"How old are your girls?"

"Natalie is six and Chrissy is four."

"Great. My Mark is seven and Jacob is five. They're at their grandmother's now, but they'll be home later. It'll be nice for them to have playmates next door. Do you work?"

"I'm the new librarian."

Gwen's smile grew bigger. "Really? That's wonderful. We've all been wondering who it would be. I can't tell you how excited the town is to finally have our own library again. The closest one is in Sawyer's Bend about twenty minutes from here. It's nice, but it's not ours. I think a library should be part of the town."

"I agree, and I have lots of ideas for programs and events to benefit the community. I want the library to be a place the residents of Dover look forward to coming."

"I'm so glad to hear that. Are you and your husband staying here with Shaw?"

"No. I mean, yes. I'm a widow. I'm only staying here temporarily." She filled her in about the purse snatching.

"That's awful. You must have been terrified. I'm glad you're all right. And I'm glad Shaw was there to help. You know he's Dover's most eligible bachelor?"

"I didn't know that." Though she wasn't surprised. It fit with what she'd heard about him.

"Every woman from here to Jackson has tried to catch him. But he's not about to be caught. He's too content being single. If we could auction him off, we'd raise enough money to fund our local charities for the next decade."

Lainie couldn't argue. Shaw was very attractive. Physically well built and handsome, but it was his character she questioned. His irresponsibility where others were concerned was a flaw she couldn't ignore.

"He only dates a woman twice, then it's over." Gwen snapped her fingers in the air to emphasize her point. "I think something or someone in his past hurt him deeply. But he's a good guy. He teaches some of the teen boys woodworking in his spare time."

Lainie wasn't sure what to make of that piece of information. Her neighbor was painting a picture of her landlord that was difficult to process. She found the contradictions unsettling.

"If you need a babysitter, just let me know. I don't work so I'm here most of the time, and I love kids. The more the merrier."

Gwen was going to be a joy to live next to and Lainie had a feeling they would quickly become close friends, even after she left Shaw's house. "I might take you up on that, if you're serious. I need to meet with the mayor on Monday to see when I can start work."

"I'd be happy to keep the girls. I'll bring the boys over later so they can get acquainted. It was so nice to meet you. Why don't you visit our church tomorrow? Peace Community on the square. We'll save you a seat."

The invitation warmed her heart. "I'd like that. I want to get the girls back into Sunday chool." Gwen gave her the time of the service then said goodbye, leaving a smile on Lainie's face. Her visions of small-town life were starting to materialize. She'd had her first cozy conversation over a picket fence with a neighbor and been invited to church. She prayed the looming issues with her new job would be resolved as easily.

Returning to the porch, she watched her daughters darting in and out of the bushes and playing with the dog. Accepting Shaw's offer was turning out to be a blessing, after all. She was staying in a charming old Victorian house, her girls had a yard and a dog to play with, and now neighbors. But this home was only temporary. She prayed she could find a place as nice once the issues with her job were sorted out.

The aroma of fresh pizza permeated the cab of Shaw's truck as he drove home Saturday, reminding him how hungry he was. He and Russ had managed to get a good portion of the drywall hung on the second floor of the library before running out of materials. He couldn't get another load until Monday.

Tired and hungry, he'd stopped and picked up a couple of pizzas. One for himself and one for Lainie and the girls. He wasn't sure if she'd appreciate the gesture, but he felt guilty for leaving them alone all day. He hadn't been able to stop thinking about them. Lainie had flitted through his mind at unexpected moments, tempting him to call and check on her, but he'd held off. He understood her resistance to accepting his help. But his conscience wouldn't let him turn away. Now that he understood how alone she was, he was even more determined to protect her and the kids until the library was done and she had a job And a safe place to live. He owed them that.

Shaw carried the boxes onto the back porch and knocked on Lainie's door. He found himself looking forward to seeing her again, and curious about what she'd done all day. The frown on her face when she opened the door dampened his mood. He forced a smile anyway and held out the pizza box. "I thought you and the kids might like a pizza."

Lainie blinked. "Oh. Thank you. That was very thoughtful. I was just about to fix supper." She looked into his eyes and he saw the indecision. She was wondering how to invite him to stay. And not wanting to. The realization stung more than he'd expected. He handed her the top box.

"It's pepperoni. I didn't know if the kids like the other toppings."

Chrissy charged into the kitchen and stopped in front

of him, tilting her head back and smiling. "Hey, Misser Shaw. We played with Beaux today."

"Is that pizza for us?" Natalie glanced at her mother. "Pepperoni?"

"Yes. Won't you stay and eat with us?"

Her smile had warmed some. "No, but thanks." He raised the other box. "I got one for myself. And Beaux." He stepped back, suddenly aware of the sweet scent of her perfume, and his own end-of-the-day dirt and grime. His shirt was covered in drywall dust. "Besides, I need to clean up, and I have a lot of paperwork to catch up on. I'll see you tomorrow."

"Thanks again."

Shaw crossed the short distance to his own back door and went inside. He set the pizza on the table, his appetite fading. Russ had expressed concern about having Lainie nearby all the time. Shaw had dismissed the idea, but now he was beginning to think his friend was right. Simply knowing she was on the other side of the wall left him distracted and off balance.

He needed to lock thoughts of Lainie in the back of his mind, and tackle his bookkeeping files. Grabbing a slice of pizza, he munched it on his way to the shower. Feeling like a new man, he pulled on khaki shorts and an old T-shirt and returned to the kitchen. He loved his job, and he was proud he'd managed to start his own company. But he wasn't fond of the paperwork involved. He'd rather spend his time working with clients and overseeing the projects. He hoped to hire someone to do the books soon, but not until the library was done. Until then, he was living on a shoestring.

He'd been working about an hour when he sensed he was being watched. He glanced around, realizing his kitchen door was still open and he could see across the hall to the French door sealing off Lainie's side. Since he lived alone, he'd never thought about closing doors, but he might need to start now that he had three ladies next door who could easily peek through the glass door and see him. Movement prompted a closer look, and he saw a little face peering through one of the panes. The younger one. Chrissy. She smiled and waved at him. He waved back, feeling silly. He'd never been around little kids and wasn't sure how to handle them. Beaux rose and trotted into the hall and poked his nose at the glass. Shaw could hear Chrissy's giggles.

The little girl disappeared and Beaux returned to Shaw's side. It was going to be interesting having them in his house. He focused his attention on the computer screen again, but he'd barely started on his task, when he heard a knock on the back door. He was surprised to see Lainie on the other side. "Hey. What's up? You okay?" She wouldn't come to his side without a good reason.

"I hate to bother you when you're working, but the sink is stopped up, and I can't find a plunger. Could you take a look at it?"

"Sure. I'll get my snake and be right there."

When he entered Lainie's kitchen a few minutes later, she was staring at Natalie with a stern expression and her arms crossed.

"Why would you do that?"

The little girl shrugged. "It was dirty and I wanted to clean it. It fell down the hole. I didn't mean to."

Shaw looked at Lainie. "What's wrong?"

"My daughter tried to wash her fuzzy bracelet in the sink."

Shaw frowned. He wasn't sure what a fuzzy bracelet might look like, but if it was stuck in the drain, he
could get it out. "No problem. We'll get it out and have
your sink working in no time."

Lainie sent Natalie to her room with instructions
to take her sister with her and get ready for bed. "I'm
so sorry."

"This is an old house and something always needs
fixed. This sink drain should have a cover. I never noticed that before." He started feeding the slender wire
snake down the drain. "I guess everything went okay
today?"

"Yes. I met your neighbor."

"Gwen and Eric are good people. We attend the same
church."

"You go to church?"

Shaw wasn't sure if he should be hurt or angry at her
surprise. He shot a glance at her over his shoulder. "Just
a sinner saved by grace." Her lack of response told him
she regretted her comment.

"So, how is the library coming along?"

He knew what Lainie really wanted to know. Had he
made significant progress today? She wanted to make
sure he was keeping on task. Shaw pulled out the snake.
Whatever was clogging the drain was wedged in the
trap. He pulled a wrench from his tool box and sat on
the floor, opening the cabinet doors to work on the
pipes. "We hit another snag. Russ and I will have to do
the drywall ourselves. We can't find a crew available
to do the job."

"What does that mean?'

"Several days' delay. Can you get me a bucket?"

"What?"

"I have to take the trap off. I need something to catch the water."

"Oh. I think I saw one in the laundry room."

She returned quickly with the bucket. He lay down under the sink, stretching his legs across the floor as he fought the rusty pipe. "Don't worry, Lainie. I'll stay on top of the project. I want it done on time as much as you do." He put all his strength behind the wrench and pulled. The joint finally broke free. A stream of brown water and a thick glob of slimy junk plopped into the bucket.

"I doubt that."

Shaw tugged himself from under the sink, staring up at Lainie from the floor. "If I don't complete this job on time, I'll have to pay a fine that will probably bankrupt my company. So yes, I do have as much to lose as you do if I fail."

He hadn't meant to sound angry. But he was painfully aware of the looming deadline and what he had to lose. The setback with the drywall hadn't helped. Moving back under the sink, he reconnected the trap and stood. It would need to be replaced with plastic pipes soon, but it should hold for a while.

He ran water through the sink to make sure the drain flowed freely. "Good as new." He stepped back and found Lainie staring at him.

"Is that true?" she asked. "Could you lose your business if the construction isn't done in time?"

"Those are the terms of the contract I signed. I've got four weeks to finish and six weeks of work yet to do."

"I didn't know."

"No reason you should."

"Do you think you can finish in time?"

"It'll mean pulling some all-nighters, but I have no choice. I need to finish. My future depends on it. It's not just the fine. It's my reputation that would be ruined. The people here would never trust me again. I've worked too hard to mess that up."

Lainie studied him a moment as if she were contemplating what he'd told her. "Thank you for fixing the sink."

"You're welcome. There'll probably be more repairs to do. Like I said, it's an old house." He thought he saw a hint of understanding in her eyes. Hope took root. He wanted to see more than understanding. He wanted to see friendship, anything other than condemnation.

"Hey, Misser Shaw." Chrissy hurried over to him as he dried his hands on a paper towel. "Did you find my sister's fuzzy bracelet?"

"Uh, yes, but I don't think it's any good anymore." He pointed to the bucket on the floor filled with brown gunk.

"Ew." Chrissy pinched her nose against the smell.

"Thanks for the pizza, Mister Shaw." Natalie grinned up at him from her mother's side.

"My pleasure."

"Girls, it's bedtime. Say good-night and go back upstairs. I'll be up in a minute."

"Night, Mister Shaw." Natalie smiled full out, flashing her twin dimples.

Chrissy came to his side and grinned. She placed her hand over her mouth, made a kissing sound, then blew it toward him. "Night. See you in the morning."

Shaw watched the girls scurry up the stairs, a strange warmth curling inside his chest. He wasn't sure if he liked the sensation or not. Gathering up his tools and the bucket of water, he said good-night and returned to his side of the house.

He liked helping people. He enjoyed working with the teens he taught. He welcomed the chance to aid the members of his church. But helping Lainie tonight had been a different experience. He'd felt like a knight coming to the rescue and receiving a boon in the form of a kiss blown by a tiny girl with glasses.

Shaw rubbed his forehead. He was obviously exhausted and not thinking clearly. He closed his kitchen door, snapped his fingers at Beaux, then headed into the bedroom. He needed sleep. But he had a feeling Lainie and two little charmers with blond hair and blue eyes would be invading his dreams tonight.

Chapter Four

Lainie pulled the brush through Natalie's curly hair trying to be gentle, but her daughter still winced.

"Ow. Mommy, you pull too hard."

"Sorry, sweetie, but we're running late for church and I still have to fix your sister's hair. Do you want a bow?" Natalie nodded and darted off to find one.

Lainie called to Chrissy and picked up a small rubber band.

"Mommy, can I have two tails today?"

"Sure." Her youngest liked her hair out of her eyes. She pulled the silky blond hair into sections, one over each ear, before placing a kiss on the top of the little head. Downstairs, Lainie picked up her makeup-bag purse, her gaze drifting to the sink Shaw had fixed last night.

He'd answered his door, and she'd found herself keenly aware of him—as a man. Obviously fresh from a shower, his hair had been damp and combed back, making his dark blue eyes even more noticeable. He had smelled clean, brisk, like soap. He'd been earthy and masculine, and she'd found herself in an odd tug-of-war—wanting to flee and wanting to linger.

She'd returned to her kitchen, determined to ignore her reactions, only to find new things to disturb her when he'd started work on her sink. He'd been confident and capable as he'd gone about his task. His muscles had bunched and strained as he worked with the wrench, his long legs stretched across her kitchen floor. But the thing that stuck in her mind most now was his admission that he had as much invested in completing the library as she did. She needed the employment. He needed to ensure the future of his business. For some reason, that knowledge gave her a measure of comfort. Not that she was concerned for his company—hardly— but she at least had the comfort of knowing he'd do all he could to make sure the deadline was met.

They arrived at church later than she would have liked, which wasn't unusual for them. Getting the girls ready and out the door was always a challenge. Finding no parking spaces near the church, she drove down the block, angling the car into a slot along the courthouse park.

Gwen was waiting on the front sidewalk of the stately red brick church when they arrived. She waved and smiled. "I'm so glad you came. I've saved you a seat."

Lainie took the bulletin the greeter handed her and stepped inside the old church. An air of reverence and tranquility wrapped around her the moment she crossed the threshold. Her church attendance had suffered during the past few months. Closing out her old job and getting ready for the move to Dover had consumed all her time and energy. It felt good to be back in a worship environment again.

Gwen stopped midway down the aisle and pointed to a pew on the left. "We saved this section behind us for you. We've got a full house today."

Lainie guided the girls in first, reminding them to be quiet and sit still. Her gaze traveled around the historic edifice, admiring the richly stained arched buttresses, the massive pipe organ and vivid liturgy cloths placed on the pulpit. Peace Community Church was vastly different from the church they'd attended in Memphis, which had been a more modern style of building.

Closing her eyes, she thanked the Lord for providing such a beautiful sanctuary in which to worship. Her moment was interrupted by a fidgety Natalie. Reaching across Chrissy, Lainie tapped her daughter's knee and whispered, "Please sit still." Lainie opened the bulletin and read the contents, excited about the various programs and events coming up. As soon as she was working, she'd sign up for some of them.

The prelude had just begun when she became aware of someone nearby.

"May I join you?"

She glanced up to see Shaw standing in the aisle, a small smile softening his angled jawline and warming the dark blue eyes. She slid over to make room, immediately regretting it when the spicy scent of his aftershave penetrated her senses and sparked an awareness of her landlord she didn't welcome. The girls leaned around her and waved frantically at him. He smiled and waved back. She gently pressed their hands down into their laps. She wasn't surprised to see Shaw here. He said he attended, but she hadn't expected him to sit with her. Her awareness of him grew with each passing moment.

He looked different this morning. She was accustomed to seeing the rugged contractor in work boots and jeans. Last night, he'd been the earthy, freshly showered to-the-rescue handyman. Today, he was clean shaven and professional in dark gray trousers and dress shirt, the rolled-up sleeves revealing his tan skin and the shiny watch around his wrist. She glanced at him and found him staring at her with his probing navy eyes. Embarrassed to be caught staring, she looked away, trying to ignore the heat in her cheeks.

The organist began to play as the choir filed in, and the congregation stood and sang an old hymn. Thankfully, the words were displayed on a screen behind the pulpit, preventing her from having to share a hymnal with Shaw. But the sound of his rich baritone stilled her voice. He sang with conviction, as if he believed every word of the hymn. She fought the urge to peek at him, not wanting to risk eye contact again. He wasn't the man she'd expected. And she wasn't sure how she felt about it. Oh, he was a handsome, compelling man. No argument there. She could easily understand why he was the target of every single female in the area. Shaw possessed that heart-tugging appeal women were drawn to. But not her.

Lainie focused all her attention on the service, finding her spirit soothed as she released her worries into the Lord's care. The liturgy was more traditional than her old congregation, but she welcomed the connection to others who worshipped in this historic church.

Reverend Jim Barrett proved to be a powerful speaker, and Lainie lost herself in the teaching he presented. When the pastor read a passage from Psalm 139, the words pierced deep into her spirit.

"Search me, God, and know my heart; test me and know my anxious thoughts."

The Lord had been nudging her for some time to confront issues from her past, but she'd ignored Him. Plumbing the depths of her emotions was too painful a task. Still, maybe it was time she looked inside herself and took an honest inventory.

Surrounded by the peace of the old sanctuary, Lainie saw how her grief had allowed seeds of bitterness to grow. She'd become isolated and withdrawn. She wanted to be happy again, to enjoy life fully and let go of the past. But if she did, she'd be forgetting her children's father, dismissing their life together, brief as it had been, as if it hadn't mattered. No. She had to hold on. Never let go. It would be a betrayal.

The benediction ended and Shaw stepped into the aisle to let her and the girls exit.

Gwen joined them, patting Shaw on the back and smiling at Lainie. Gwen's husband, Eric, spoke to Shaw as they made their way toward the front of the church, where the pastor and his wife waited to greet everyone. As they approached the last pew, a woman stepped forward and gave Gwen a hug.

"Lainie, I'd like you to meet my mother, Mrs. Adams. Mom, this is Lainie Hollings and her girls. Natalie and Chrissy."

Instead of the smile Lainie expected, the woman's eyes narrowed into an angry glare.

"I saw your picture in the paper this morning. I know who you are."

The woman's harsh tone made the hairs on Lainie's arm stand up. "Paper?"

Gwen touched her arm. "The Sunday edition of the

Dover Dispatch ran a wonderful article about you being our new librarian. It was very flattering. I meant to tell you."

Shaw stepped closer to her side, squaring his shoulders as if preparing to defend her.

Mrs. Adams raised her chin, the chill in her eyes still shooting icy daggers. "It said this is your first position as a librarian. I'm sure our new facility would benefit from someone with more experience."

"Mother." Gwen blushed and attempted to pull her away, but the woman stood still.

Lainie wasn't sure what was going on, but she knew she had to correct the misconception. "That's not true, Mrs. Adams. I've worked at libraries many years before getting my degree."

"I don't see why the board felt it necessary to hire an outsider when we have a perfectly qualified person here in Dover who has years of experience and the *respect* of every resident in town."

Lainie's chest tightened. Hot stinging humiliation rose along her neck and into her cheeks. Her stomach twisted into a knot. Shaw placed his hand on her back, muttered something to Gwen and her mother, then firmly guided her and the girls out a side entrance to the parking lot.

"I was afraid this might happen,"

Lainie glanced at him. "What? I don't understand. Why was she so upset? What have I done?"

"Nothing. It's not you exactly."

"Then what exactly?"

Natalie tugged on her hand. "Mommy, why was that lady mad at you?"

Chrissy joined in. "Yeah, she was mean. I don't like her."

"Not now, girls. We'll talk about it later." She sent a confused glance at Shaw. How did she explain something to her children when she didn't understand herself?

"Where are you parked?"

"Along the courthouse park."

Shaw walked with them across the street into the park, stopping near a small pond. Slipping his hand into his pocket, he pulled out coins and handed them to the girls. "Ladies, this pond has a lot of hungry fish in it, and if you put these coins into the machine beside it, it'll give you fish food."

Lainie nodded her permission and the girls ran off. Shaw guided her to a bench nestled in the shade of a sprawling old live oak tree.

He watched the children for a moment before he spoke. "Russ called me this morning to tell me about the article in the paper."

Lainie braced herself. "Was it bad?"

"Not at all. The problem is the town was expecting someone else to be the new librarian."

"Who?"

Shaw explained about the affection the town held for the former librarian, but it did little to soothe her hurt feelings. "It's not like I campaigned against this woman. The board hired me because of my qualifications. I thought small towns were supposed to be friendly and welcoming."

"They are. They're also loyal, and they see themselves as being loyal to one of their own."

"Is that why you've been standing guard like a

watchdog this morning?" The grin he gave her caused a skip in her heartbeat.

"Is that what I'm doing?"

"You practically forced yourself to sit with us, then you hovered like a bodyguard as we were leaving the sanctuary."

Shaw frowned and nodded. "Guess I did. After I heard about the article I thought I'd better try and run interference for you."

"Why didn't you warn me sooner?"

"You've been through a lot. Your welcome to Dover hasn't been very kind, and I hated to add more to your burden."

"But you suspected I'd get a cool reception at church?"

"Yes. Though I was praying the members would display a little more Christian charity."

"Most of them did."

He leaned closer. "It'll be all right. Give it some time. The announcement caught a lot of folks off guard."

She nodded. "I suppose. My feelings are hurt, that's all."

Shaw smiled and lightly touched her arm. "Anyone ever tell you you're a tough lady?"

"I've had to be." She'd intended the comment to put him in his place and remind him of the past, but her moment of triumph faded quickly at the deep sadness that darkened his eyes.

"Trust me. Once the citizens of Dover get to know you, they'll come around."

Trust Shaw? Not likely.

He stood. "If everything here is good, I have an appointment I need to get to."

"Big date?" Why had she asked that question? His personal life was none of her business.

"No. Big job. My other projects are suffering because of the library. I'm trying to get caught up." He glanced at the girls then nodded at her. "I'll see you at home later."

Lainie waited until Shaw was driving off in his truck before calling a halt to her daughters' fish feeding. She hoped he was right about the people of Dover eventually accepting her. Perhaps it would help if she made herself more visible and started to meet people. A friendly smile and showing sincere interest in their town could go a long way to breaking the ice and shifting people's negative reaction to her new position.

As she finished fastening Chrissy into her car seat, Lainie spotted a newspaper dispenser a few feet away. Curious to read the article written about her, she inserted the required coins and pulled out the weekend edition of the *Dover Dispatch*.

By the time she'd stopped at the grocery and returned to the house, she was relieved to see Shaw's truck was gone. She changed her clothes, then went downstairs and opened the paper. The article about her was very nice. It mentioned her years of working in libraries, her degree and her children. Other than being a newcomer to Dover, there was nothing in the piece that should have upset anyone. Except for the fact that the residents had expected Millie to get the job. Well, she'd have to prove to them she was the perfect one to run their new library. And she would, as soon as she could start work.

"Mommy, I'm hungry. Can we have hot dogs?"

An idea blossomed in Lainie's mind. Gwen had told her about Friendship Park, where the people liked to gather on weekends. She'd said there were hiking trails, picnic areas, playgrounds and ball fields. It was a beautiful Sunday afternoon. What better way to meet the locals than at a place called Friendship Park?

"Girls, how would you like to go to the park?"

She would take the initiative and reach out to the locals. If she was friendly and open then maybe they would see that she wasn't a threat, simply a newcomer who wanted to fit in and bring the joy of the new library to Dover.

Monday afternoon, Lainie stepped into the mayor's office fighting to maintain a professional demeanor. The balding, fifty-something man had a warm smile and a firm handshake, which bolstered her hopes. He listened attentively, but when she finished, the frown on his face raised her anxiety.

"I understand and sympathize with the position you are in, Mrs. Hollings, but there's not much I can do for you. No one is allowed to work in that building until it's completed and passed inspection. It's not safe. And I know for a fact Shaw McKinney is a stickler for safety."

Lainie bit off the contradictory comment she wanted to make. Shaw might be a stickler for safety now, but where had that concern been when her husband was on that steeply pitched roof?

"Mayor, with all due respect, I cannot be unemployed for weeks. I have two children to support."

"Believe me, I wish I could help you, but it's out of my hands. Our first concern is the completion of the facility. If the building is not finished on time and in the manner prescribed, the city of Dover must assume the cost of running the library. Unfortunately, we're not in a position to do that. We must adhere to the directives in this bequest or lose the library."

"Couldn't you speak with the donor and explain the situation?"

"I don't know who he or she is. Our benefactor wishes to remain anonymous. The donation was a way of housing their personal book collection. I think the stringent specifications stem from this person's desire to ensure the building will do their books justice."

While she sympathized with his position, that didn't help her situation. She'd have to find a job. Quick. "I understand, Mayor. However, I would have appreciated some notification so I could have made other arrangements. I came to Dover prepared to start work."

"I apologize for that. It was an oversight. But I promise you, I'll let you know the moment things are ready."

As Lainie walked through the old courthouse, she searched for a way to make ends meet for the next few weeks. She was not going to live off Shaw for a month until she could start work at the library.

She pushed open the old wooden door and stepped outside into the warm sunshine and a welcome breeze. As her eyes adjusted to the light, she saw Shaw jogging up the stone steps. "What are you doing here? It's the middle of the day." There was a hopeful look on his face that intensified his cobalt eyes.

"I wanted to know how it went."

"Not good. There's nothing he can do until the building is completed. Something about the conditions of the donation."

Shaw nodded. "I was afraid of that. I've had to navigate a maze of oddball construction requirements to accommodate the building design. Even with the structural problems, I could have been finished with the job weeks ago if it hadn't been for the details required." A small smile moved his mouth. "I guess it's up to me now."

"I can't wait that long." She glanced around the square. There were plenty of shops and businesses. Maybe she could get a job with one of them. "I used to wait tables. I could work at the diner part-time."

"I may have another suggestion. Come to work for me."

Lainie frowned. "I don't know anything about construction."

"That's not what I had in mind." He glanced over her shoulder. "Let's grab something to drink and I'll tell you my idea."

A cool glass of tea sounded wonderful. She could use a few moments to process the meeting, but she didn't have the time. "I can't. I need to get back to the girls. Gwen is watching them for me. What kind of job are you suggesting?"

"I need a bookkeeper. Between the library job and my other projects, I don't have much time to stay on top of my business accounts and I'm falling behind. If I had someone to handle the paperwork, it would free me up to spend more time on the job. I'd pay you a fair salary and you could work from the house so you wouldn't need a babysitter. And you'd have free rent."

It was a tempting offer, but the thought of being further indebted to Shaw didn't set well. If she said yes, she'd still be taking his help, but at least she'd be earning her own money. She wasn't too proud to remain his tenant. She'd scanned the homes and apartments for rent section of the Sunday paper, and been shocked and disappointed at the prices. She'd expected the cost of living to be cheaper in a small town. "I don't know."

Shaw smiled. "Think about it. We'll talk tonight, and I'll show you what I need you to do. It would help both of us, Lainie."

She looked into his blue eyes and saw that hopeful glint again. "I'll think about it. But that's all I can promise."

"Fair enough. I'd better get back to work. We should get the drywall upstairs done today."

As she drove home, Lainie thought about Shaw's offer. Without a paycheck, there was little she could do but rely on Shaw for everything she needed. Once her new credit cards arrived, she could use them for her expenses, though she couldn't live off them. She'd deliberately set low limits. Working for Shaw would draw her deeper into Shaw's debt, and his life, but it was a practical solution in the short term.

Lainie parked the car in Shaw's driveway, then made her way next door to pick up the girls. Gwen greeted her with a big smile and the offer of a glass of sweet tea. Settled on Gwen's expansive back deck, Lainie felt some of the afternoon's tension ease.

"How's it going? Are you getting settled in?"

Lainie shrugged. "Coming to Dover was supposed to be a new start for us, and it's not working out at all the way I'd hoped. I took the girls to Friendship Park yesterday. I thought it would be a good way to meet some of the locals. But all I got were stares and a few curt comments. So much for the small town with the big heart."

"I'm sorry. Try not to get too discouraged. Once the library opens and everyone sees how wonderful you are, and all the programs you'll start, they'll forget about you being a newcomer." Gwen squeezed her hand. "The people of Dover are wonderful, loving and generous at heart. We have our sour apples and a few angry malcontents, but that's true of every town. I'm sorry you're not getting the warm welcome you expected, but I promise you they will come around. In their minds, you've attacked one of their beloved citizens. They're standing up for her and they'll do the same for you once they get to know you." She picked up a gift bag from a small table and handed it to her. "Maybe this will cheer you up."

"For me? What is it?" Lainie removed the paper filler from the bright green gift bag and pulled out a lovely leather shoulder bag.

"It's a combination welcome to Dover and apology gift. For my mother's horrible behavior at church yesterday."

Lainie stopped with her hand on the purse zipper. "Oh, Gwen, you didn't have to do this. But it's lovely."

"I know you're trying to make do, but no woman feels complete without a purse. I thought this would be the prefect size. It's small, but still large enough for a bag of cookies or a book."

"Books." Lainie's mind kicked into gear. "Books. What about all the books? Why didn't I ask him?"

"What are you talking about?"

"The library books. The mayor said the person who donated the library did so to preserve their personal book collection. Where are they? And what about the new books? Have they been ordered? Finishing the building is great, but if there aren't any books, it's useless. I need to call the mayor." Lainie gave Gwen a big hug then called for the girls and hurried them out the door. "Thank you for the purse. It's perfect."

After sending Natalie and Chrissy to play in the Princess Club, Lainie dialed the Mayor's office only to learn he was in a meeting for the remainder of the day. The secretary suggested she attend the Library Board meeting the next evening and discuss her problem with them then.

Renewed hope bubbled up from deep inside. Maybe she could convince the board to let her work on the books. Unless there was some weird stipulation that forbade it. She was grateful to the anonymous donor for their gift, but the strings attached to it were bothersome.

So far, her arrival in Dover had been fraught with speed bumps and detours, but she refused to sit by and twiddle her thumbs for the next three to four weeks waiting for Shaw McKinney to finish his part of the project. There was too much at stake for her and her girls.

In the meantime, she might need to seriously consider his offer to work for him. If she failed to sway the library board, then at least she'd have income and a roof over her head.

And she did like staying in this old house.

Chapter Five

The soft evening breeze drifted through the small window above the kitchen sink was enticing Lainie outside to sit on the porch and watch the evening fade. If she took Shaw's offer to work for him and remained in this house, the first thing she'd do would be to find some comfy chairs for the front porch. She longed to enjoy the porch swing out front, but she was reluctant to ask her landlord if it was okay. Keeping clear lines between them was wise.

Pushing the start button on the dishwasher, she wiped her hands on a dish towel then stepped onto the back porch to check on the girls. She'd allowed them to stay outside a little longer tonight. They finally had a big yard to play in and she wanted them to enjoy it as much as possible. Scanning the lush yard, she frowned when she couldn't see either child. "Natalie. Chrissy." A finger of fear touched her spine. A list of horrible possibilities flashed through her mind. Her girls were her life. If anything happened to them she couldn't go on.

Losing her husband so suddenly had left her with a deep-seated fear of losing her children to some un-

known catastrophe. Her mother had helped her overcome much of her fear by reminding her frequently
that the Lord was in charge. But sometimes the fear
would break loose, threatening to overwhelm her ratio-
nal mind. She called out again, her voice rising in pitch.

"We're in here, Mommy."

She spun around to see Chrissy's face poking out
from Beaux's pet door. Relief made her slightly light-
headed. "What are you doing?"

"I fit in the door like Beaux does."

Her delighted smile washed away Lainie's fear. She
did look cute on her hands and knees in the small opening. Still, she couldn't condone their being in Shaw's
side of the house without telling her. "Where is your
sister? And why are you in Mr. Shaw's house?"

"Beaux invited us in."

Chrissy pulled back through the opening and Lainie
tapped on the door. Chrissy opened it and smiled, pushing her glasses up.

"We are going to have a serious talk, young lady."

Lainie found Natalie seated on the kitchen floor tugging on Beaux's ears.

Natalie muttered a soft *uh-oh* when she saw her
mother. Shaw was seated at his kitchen table in front
of his laptop. He had an odd look on his face, but she
couldn't decide if he was upset or simply amused.

"Girls, you know better than to bother Mr. Shaw.
Especially when he's working."

"We wanted to help Beaux." Natalie rested her head
against the dog's side.

"He was lonely." Chrissy darted to the dog and fell
to her knees, wrapping her little arms around his spot-

ted neck. If Lainie didn't know better, she'd think the dog was laughing at Chrissy.

Shaw stifled a smile and Lainie felt her tension ease. "I'm so sorry. I'll have a talk with them."

"It's all right. They saved me from trying to juggle any more numbers." He rubbed the bridge of his nose and exhaled a weary sigh. "I know it's not complicated, but I'm too tired to make sense of anything tonight."

She stepped to his side, glancing at the computer screen, resisting the urge to place a comforting hand on his shoulder. This was as good a time as any to tell him what she'd decided. "I've been thinking about your suggestion."

His eyes brightened. "And?"

"I'd like to accept."

"Great. I really need your help on this."

She forced herself to look away from his eyes. Certain emotions made them change from a navy blue to cobalt. They were an unusual color, and one she found far too fascinating. "I'm familiar with this program. I kept the books for my mother. She owned a small gift shop. After she passed, I went to work for a wealthy friend of hers in Memphis as her personal assistant, and she used the same program."

"That'll make things easier. When can we get together and go over the details?"

"Tonight is good. After I put the girls to bed."

He stood and extended his hand. "Then we have a deal? We'll be working together from now on."

His words had implications she wasn't sure she liked. The working part was fine. It was the together thing that sent a twinge along her nerves. She hesitated a moment before slipping her hand into his. His grasp was warm and firm, and sent a strange vibration along her senses, an odd connection of some sort. She looked into his eyes and saw her own surprise reflected in his. She tugged her hand away.

He held her gaze a moment before resting his hands on his hips and nodding. "I'll get things in order and we'll go over what I need you to do. And we'll discuss your pay." He nodded toward the French door that separated them. "Just tap on the glass when you're ready."

"Okay." She took a step back, battling the feeling she'd just made a deal with the enemy. Shaw wasn't exactly the enemy, but he wasn't a friend, either. "Girls. Let's go and let Mr. Shaw finish his work. You can play with Beaux tomorrow."

She was halfway out the door when Shaw caught up to her. His expression was serious, his eyes holding a hint of pleading.

"Lainie, this will be a good arrangement for both of us. You'll have income to tide you over, and I'll be free to devote all my time to finishing the construction."

She couldn't argue, but she felt as if she'd somehow betrayed her husband with her decision. "I know."

She consoled herself with the knowledge that her survival was her first concern. She needed to provide for her girls, and this was only a temporary solution.

Shaw stood in Lainie's kitchen Tuesday evening trying to process what she'd just said. "You want me to what?" He'd barely stepped inside the house after a tough day at work, eager to shower and chill, when Lainie tapped on the glass in the French door, beckoning him to come over. They'd got together last night and gone over his accounts. She'd caught on quickly, lifting a huge burden from his shoulders.

He'd entered her kitchen, expecting her to have questions about his business. But instead, she'd blindsided him with a request to babysit Natalie and Chrissy.

"It'll only be for an hour or so. I asked Gwen to watch them, but she and Eric have an appointment this evening. I don't know anyone else, and I can't leave them with some teenager I don't even know. I need to meet with the library board tonight. I'm sure I can convince them to let me start cataloging the benefactor's book collection."

Lainie might as well have asked him to go shopping for a prom dress. Shaw held up his hands in refusal. "No way. I don't know anything about kids."

"I wouldn't ask if it weren't important. Believe me, you are the *last* person I want to trust my children to, but you said yourself that getting this job done on time is important to both of us. The library books are a vital part of that completion, don't you think?"

Shaw scraped his knuckles along his jaw. "I thought the mayor said there was no way you could start work before the building was done."

"He did. But one thing I learned from working for Mrs. Forsythe is that there are always loopholes if you look for them. I'm praying this might be mine."

The pleading in her eyes weakened his resolve. "Are you sure you want me to watch them?"

Lainie crossed her arms over her chest. "No. I'm not, but I can't take them with me. That leaves you as my only option. They go to bed at eight. I'll have them ready. All you have to do is let them play until bedtime then remind them to brush their teeth, and hear their prayers. After that, you can relax. Mainly you're here in case anything happens."

The thought chilled his blood and a stab of guilt punctured his heart. That was the problem. What *if* something happened? He'd failed this woman once. He couldn't handle failing her again. He opened his mouth to refuse, but she placed her hand on his arm, sending a warm rush along his skin. Her soft brown eyes were lit with hope and excitement. She'd had little to rejoice about since arriving in Dover. He couldn't add more disappointment because of his fears. "Okay. But keep your phone handy. I reserve the right to bail at any moment."

The smile she flashed dissolved his unease. It was a beautiful, knee-buckling sight. He remembered it well from when she would visit her husband on a job site. He cleared his throat. "What time should I be here?"

"In about forty-five minutes?"

He nodded, then headed to his place, marveling at how he'd been hoodwinked into being a babysitter. After a quick bite and a shower, he and Beaux went next door to begin serving their sentence.

Lainie ushered them in with a smile, but Shaw could see she was nervous. Was it because of the library board or that she was leaving her girls in his care? Probably a little of both. She was putting all her hopes on this meeting. He prayed it would go well.

Natalie and Chrissy charged into the room with happy smiles for him and hugs for Beaux. It left an odd hollow in a corner of his chest. He'd always liked coming home to his empty rooms. The peace and quiet restored him after a hard day. A welcome bark and nuzzle from his canine buddy was all the greeting he needed. But having two little faces smiling at him was nice, too.

"Hello, Beaux." Lainie gave the dog a welcome scratch. "Bringing the dog was a good idea. They'll be so busy playing with him, they won't be any trouble at all."

"Come on, Beaux. Let's have a tea party." Chrissy tugged on the dog's collar and he trotted off with her.

Shaw frowned as the dog disappeared into the other room. "He was supposed to be my protection." Lainie giggled softly, tripping an extra beat in his pulse. He'd never heard her laugh. It was like wind chimes.

"They're little girls, Shaw, not alien creatures." She picked up her purse. "Thank you for doing this. I know it's a huge imposition, but think of it as another way we're working together to get the library done. I'm helping you with your accounting, and you're helping me by babysitting. And I promise I won't make a habit of it." She made a thumbs-up gesture. "Pray for a positive outcome tonight."

She had a point. He stopped her at the back door. "Lainie, I know you'll convince them."

"How do you know that?"

"You convinced me to be a babysitter. That takes some doing."

His encouraging words earned him another smile, but his confidence sagged the moment Lainie walked out the door. He was alone with two little princesses, and he had no idea how to be a knight in armor. A quick glance at his watch revealed he had an hour to keep them entertained before he could put them to bed and relax.

Setting his jaw and squaring his shoulders, he walked into the living room. The sight that greeted him convinced him he was seriously out of his element. Natalie,

Chrissy and Beaux were seated in the tower around a small table. The girls wore wide-brim hats with flowers on top, and Beaux had a purple feather boa draped around his neck. The Dalmatian looked back at him with a pitiful expression. Shaw knew exactly how he felt. "Sorry, pal. There's nothing I can do."

Two sets of blue eyes looked at him above happy smiles. Chrissy stood and darted to his side, her little hand wrapping around one of his fingers as she tugged him forward. Her hand was much smaller than her mother's, but it had a similar effect on his system.

Holding Lainie's hand yesterday had left an imprint on his skin and in his mind. For an instant, he'd thought he'd felt a jolt, a strange surge of energy shoot through his system. He'd quickly dismissed the idea as nonsense. But feeling the little fingers wrapped tightly around his was doing something to him, as well. It unleashed a rush of warmth around his heart and a depth of protectiveness he'd never experienced before.

"Come on, Misser Shaw. You can come to our tea party, too."

His heart sank. No. Not that. "I have a better idea. Why don't we go outside and toss the ball for Beaux? I'll show you some of his tricks."

Natalie shook her head. "First, tea party."

Chrissy released his fingers and reached for a small blue plastic teapot. "We need water."

"Please," Natalie added sweetly.

Shaw took the pot into the kitchen, questioning his lapse in judgment in agreeing to watch the children. He felt inadequate. Nervous. What if he failed? What if something happened and he messed up, the way he'd messed up with their father? *Lord, please keep me alert and aware. Help me keep these little girls safe until Lainie comes home.* He'd keep an eagle eye on the children. Never let them out of his sight. Shaw stared at the small blue teapot, old doubts rising to the surface of his mind. He still questioned his actions that day on the roof. He needed to make sure nothing happened tonight. A quick glance at his watch revealed he'd only been a babysitter for ten minutes. It was going to be a long night.

"Sit down, Misser Shaw, so you can have your tea and cookies."

Resigned to his fate, Shaw lowered himself to the floor sitting cross-legged as Natalie handed him a tiny cup and saucer. His hand was so large, he could barely pinch his fingers together to grasp the small handle. He watched as the girls took little sips of "tea." He raised the cup and took a sip. He felt ridiculous.

Natalie smiled at him. "Isn't our Princess Club pretty?"

Shaw took in the circular area filled with feathers, bows and other girlie things. "Very nice. But I thought you said boys weren't allowed. Except Beaux."

"You're not really a boy," Natalie explained.

"Yeah, you're more of a daddy so it's okay."

Shaw's throat tightened. Daddy? No. Not happening.

"Our daddy is in heaven." Chrissy adjusted her hat.

Natalie nodded. "Mommy has a picture in her room."

How was he supposed to respond to that? "I'm sure he was a good dad."

"I guess." Natalie shrugged. "I don't remember him."

Chrissy poured more tea into her yellow cup. "He was a superhero. Mommy said so."

The knife edge of guilt twisted deeper inside him.

His actions had cost Lainie her husband and these girls a devoted father.

Chrissy looked at him. "I want to buy a new daddy. One I can hug."

Natalie adjusted her white hat with pink flowers. "You can't buy a daddy, silly. You have to find one."

For the first time, Shaw felt the full impact of what Lainie and her children had lost. The hole left in their lives. Lainie's struggles became more apparent. But she was young and lovely, and full of determination. She'd meet someone someday who could fill those empty places and be the husband she deserved, and the daddy Natalie and Chrissy longed for.

The truth was painfully clear. He had no place in Lainie's life. He'd best keep his barriers up. He couldn't afford to let his heart care. One day, the girls would grow up and ask questions about their dad. He'd never withstand the look of horror in their eyes when they learned his role in their father's death.

Natalie picked up a pink hat and held it out. "Here, Mr. Shaw, you can wear this one."

He frowned. "That's okay. I'll pass."

"You have to have a hat for a tea party. It's a rule."

He took the floppy hat with its long trailing ribbon, then looked at the little girl. The bright sparkle in her eyes, the joy in her smile, was his downfall. How was a guy supposed to stay strong in the face of such cuteness and innocence?

The girls were miniatures of their mother. Bright, engaging and full of life, and he wanted nothing more in that moment than to make them happy. With a dejected sigh, he placed the hat on his head.

"You look bee-you-tee-ful." Chrissy clasped her small hands together and gave him a dreamy smile.

He nodded, knowing that two little princesses had taken his six-foot-two frame to the mat like a WWE champion. And he didn't really mind.

For tonight, he'd let go and lose himself in pink glitter and a pretend tea party. He scratched Beaux's ear. "You tell anyone about this and I'll deny it and ship your spotted carcass to the pound. Are we clear?" A resounding and heartfelt bark was the response.

Lainie sat in the empty meeting room Tuesday evening, clutching her folder, her stomach churning with an odd mixture of emotions—anxiety over leaving Shaw in charge of her daughters, excitement over the prospect of working with the book collection, and fear that her logic and enthusiasm might not sway the board. She shoved the doubts aside. She had to trust Shaw would keep a close eye on the girls. As far as the meeting went, she'd do her best. That was all she could do.

She'd spent the day working on Shaw's books. His accounts weren't in bad shape, just behind. She'd gained a better understanding of his business. He was balancing multiple projects, any one of which could fall apart suddenly and leave him in financial trouble. She couldn't decide if he was a risk taker or just a man in the throes of starting a new business. In her job for Mrs. Forsythe, she'd helped the older woman start several small businesses and dismantle a few when they didn't work out.

The door abruptly opened and Mayor Ogden and two others walked in. The look of surprise on the mayor's face told her he hadn't been forewarned of her presence. "I thought we covered your position yesterday, Mrs. Hollings."

"We did, but I have questions about another aspect of the library I'd like to discuss with the board."

"Very well. However, you'll have to wait until we get our regular business out of the way. Let me introduce you to the other board members, Angie Durrant and Blake Prescott."

Mrs. Durrant welcomed her with a smile and a warm handshake. "You're Shaw's friend. I'm so glad to finally meet our new head librarian." Angela Durrant was an attractive woman in her fifties, with a friendly smile that made Lainie like her immediately. The other member was a man in his midthirties. Confident, polished and attractive, but distant and guarded.

Lainie's mind wandered as the business part of their meeting unfolded. She wondered how Shaw was doing with the girls. Maybe she should call and check on them. He'd looked terrified when she'd asked him to babysit. Maybe her concern should be for his safety. Her little treasures could be a handful.

She was puzzled at how quickly the girls had taken to him. She'd heard children had good instincts about people. If that was true, then Shaw wasn't all bad. If she looked at things objectively, she had no reason to distrust him. He'd been nothing but helpful from the start, and working for him had given her a sense of purpose she'd lost after the robbery and the setback with her job.

The memory of shaking Shaw's hand replayed unexpectedly in her mind. She'd found herself lingering in his grasp, surprised at the odd flutter in her pulse. His touch had been warm and secure, and given her a sense of grounding deep inside she hadn't felt for a long time.

"Now, Mrs. Hollings. What did you wish to discuss with us?" The mayor motioned her toward a chair near their conference table.

"I wanted to ask about the books." She opened her folder.

Mayor Ogden frowned and peered over the rim of his glasses. "I don't understand."

"The donor's private collection. Is it here in town? Has anyone started to sort them? And what about the other books the library will need? Who selected them? Has that process even begun?" The board members stared back at her. "Everyone seems to be focused on getting the building finished, but no one has mentioned what's to go inside once it's done."

Angie Durrant glanced at the mayor. "That's a very good question. As I understand it, the collection is housed in a warehouse in town until it's time to be transferred to the library."

"I hope the warehouse is climate controlled, otherwise the books could suffer damage."

Mayor Ogden harrumphed. "As for the rest of the books, they are to be ordered by the head librarian."

"Which is me. So when can I start? I'd like to see what books are included in the donation so I can decide what needs to be purchased for a well-rounded selection. I'd like to review the budget, as well, to see how many books I can order and how many employees I can hire."

"Wait just a minute, Mrs. Hollings. You aren't even on the payroll. We can't authorize anything like that until the building is done. And the project is behind schedule."

"Exactly. Was there no provision for that? How were the books supposed to be processed if the job had been on schedule?" The members glanced at one another.

Lainie took a second to tamp down her rising irritation. Didn't these people understand what they were facing? "May I ask how you planned on opening a library without any books?"

Angie Durrant turned to the man on her left. "Blake, you're the legal advisor here. Mrs. Hollings raises a good point."

Blake, who had been silent so far, straightened in his chair. "If the remodel had been completed by the initial deadline, then there would have been ample time for the books to be moved in and the remainder ordered and delivered. With the deadline pushed back, there were no provisions for adjustments in other areas."

Lainie was beginning to think this bequest was more trouble than it was worth in some ways. "So what happens now? You'll have a grand opening for an empty library?" Lainie leaned toward the members, pressing her point. "The books in the donor's collection have to be entered into the library system individually by hand. That takes time."

"What do you suggest?"

Lainie appreciated Angie Durrant's genuine interest. "Let me start work on that now. Mr. McKinney assures me he'll have the construction done before the deadline. If I can start cataloging the book collection and start ordering the rest of the stock, then we can finish at the same time."

Angie Durrant sent Lainie an encouraging smile. "She has a point, Bill."

Mayor Ogden huffed and tapped the table with his finger. "She cannot work until that building is done. It's not just the bequest, it's the law. There's no way around it."

"What if I could find another place to work? I could start on the books, Shaw can keep working on the building and when it's done, we simply move the books into place."

"That's a good idea." Angie smiled at Lainie.

The mayor tapped the table top with one finger. "But is it in compliance with the donation? We cannot do anything that will jeopardize this bequest."

Blake clasped his hands on the table. "That's true, Mayor, but maybe I can find something that will allow us to give Mrs. Hollings the ability to work in another capacity. I'll look into it."

"Fine." The mayor waved a hand. "Blake will contact us if he finds a solution. In the meantime, things remain as they are. Thank you for your input, Mrs. Hollings." The mayor stood and exited the room. Blake followed with a smile and a nod in her direction. Angie Durrant stopped and offered her hand.

"I think we made a wise choice when we selected you as our new librarian. Your passion for the job is evident. I'll do a little checking on my own, and keep a fire at Blake's feet and let you know when I hear something. Give me your phone number and I'll call you myself."

"Well, I must admit it's partly driven by need. I have two little girls to support. I'm living off charity at the moment and I don't like it."

"That's right. I heard Shaw was taking care of you. He's a good man. We think the world of him."

Everyone in Dover seemed to think that. Apparently, she was the only one who knew a different side to him. Or were they right and she was wrong? She didn't have time or energy to think about that now.

Inside her vehicle, Lainie pulled out her phone and dialed Shaw's number, needing reassurance that things had gone well. The phone rang several times before going to voice mail, triggering a small grain of concern. Maybe he hadn't made it to the phone in time to answer. She dialed again. Still no answer.

With her heart in her throat, she started the car and headed home. The urgency in her veins cried out to break the speed limits, but common sense ruled. It was only a few blocks, after all. But what if something had happened? What if one of the girls was ill or hurt and Shaw had taken them to the hospital? Losing her girls was the only thing that turned her from a practical, commonsense woman into a panic-stricken jellyfish. Why hadn't he called? Surely, he wasn't that irresponsible. But he had been in the past.

Lainie stomped on the brake, bringing her car to an abrupt halt beside Shaw's truck. Grabbing her things, she jogged to the porch and hurried into the kitchen. Her heart pounded violently, but not so loudly that she didn't notice the quiet in her apartment. Were the girls in bed? If Shaw's truck was here, then nothing bad must have happened. She didn't smell smoke.

Taking a deep breath, she dashed into the living room, stopping in surprise at the sight that greeted her. Shaw was sitting in the middle of the sofa, head resting on the back, sound asleep. Chrissy was tucked up at his side, her princess crown askew on her head as she slept. Natalie was stretched out on the floor using Beaux as a pillow. The sight of the three of them brought a smile to her face. But what really tickled her were the small glitter stickers on Shaw's cheeks. From the looks of things, all was well.

She couldn't wait to hear the story behind that. Gently, she tapped his knee. He stirred then jerked awake.

"Lainie."

"Did the girls wear you out?"

He sat up, careful not to waken Chrissy. "No. They were great."

"I expected to find them asleep in their beds. Not down here."

He gave her a sheepish glance. "Yeah, well I put them in bed, but they wouldn't stay there."

Lainie giggled. "I know what you mean. I'd better get them upstairs." She scooped up Chrissy.

"I'll help." He picked up Natalie, and they went upstairs and tucked the sleeping girls into bed.

Back in the kitchen, Lainie faced Shaw. "Thank you for helping tonight."

"No problem, but I'm glad you're back." He grinned and tugged on his ear. "They're more active than my dog. Taking care of them is a huge responsibility. I don't envy you."

"Too much responsibility for a bachelor?"

"Way too much."

For some reason, Lainie was disappointed by his response.

"Did you win your case with the board?"

She smiled. "I think so. I'll know soon. The problem stems from not being allowed to work in the library until it's finished."

"No one can until the final inspection is approved and we're issued the Certificate of Occupancy."

"I pointed out flaws in their process and a possible solution. Their attorney, Blake Prescott, is looking into it."

Shaw scratched his cheek and found the stickers. He pulled them off, a blush of embarrassment staining his tanned skin. "The girls promised they'd go to bed as soon as I put on stickers."

Lainie smiled. "Didn't work, did it?" He shook his head. "They can be very inventive when they don't want to go to bed. I imagine having you and Beaux to play with was too much fun to waste on sleep."

Shaw fisted his hands and stared at them a moment before opening them and showing her his fingernails. "How do I get this stuff off?"

"Oh, my." She couldn't stop laughing at the sight of this rugged guy sporting blue nail polish. "You are a pushover, aren't you? Sit down." She took the bottle of nail polish remover from the cupboard, along with several cotton balls. "It was nice of you to let them paint you up."

"They were having fun so—"

"Give me your hand." Shaw complied, but when she took his fingers in her hand, a flash of heat darted along her arm and lodged in the center of her chest. She forced herself to look only at the nail she was working on and not his face. But with each swipe of the cotton ball, she grew more and more conscious of how nice his hands were. The broad palms, the long tapered fingers, the smooth tanned skin marred by a few scars and calluses. A workingman's hands.

Touching him stirred an unwelcome attraction. She was impressed with his willingness to let the girls cover him in stickers and paint his fingernails. She wouldn't have expected that from a diehard bachelor. Aware of the tension between them, Lainie cleared her throat and attempted light conversation. "My girls can be very persuasive."

"A couple of little charmers. It's hard to say no. They told me this sky color matched my eyes."

"Oh, no. Your eyes aren't sky blue, they're cobalt like those old bottles…" She froze. What was wrong with her? She shouldn't be paying Shaw any compliments. What would he think?

"I'm partial to brown eyes myself."

She had brown eyes. Lainie pressed her lips together, forcing herself to not react. That was the Shaw she'd expected, always looking for a way to charm the ladies. Picking up a fresh cotton ball, she doused it with polish remover and started on Shaw's other hand working quickly to complete the task.

"I'm sure the library board will decide in your favor."

"You sound confident."

"I am. Anyone who can raise two great kids all alone can do anything."

Lainie finished cleaning the last nail and released his hand, trying to ignore the compliments he'd given her. They didn't mean anything. He scattered flattery like beads at Mardi Gras, without any real thought. Still, she found herself wishing he'd meant them. Which was completely out of line. She needed some space. "Thank you again."

Shaw stood. "My pleasure. If you need a babysitter, you know where to find me. Just tap on the glass and I'll come running."

"Thanks, but I don't think I'll be needing you anymore." His eyes darkened again, and he turned to leave. A funny hitch in her pulse refused to stop, even after he'd closed the door. She needed to get a grip. She would not fall prey to the compliments of a skilled charmer like Shaw.

Chapter Six

Shaw poured a tall glass of sweet tea before sitting down in front of his laptop. A quick check revealed Lainie was staying on top of his accounts. He leaned back in the chair and smiled. One less thing to lose sleep over. Beaux laid his snout on Shaw's knee, earning a gentle scratch. His gaze drifted to the French door across the hall. It was late Wednesday night. There would be no cute faces peeking at him and waving little fingers. And no glimpse of Lainie.

He smiled when he noticed slivers of blue polish still clinging to his cuticles. Babysitting Natalie and Chrissy last night had opened a new world for him. The two little girls enchanted him as nothing ever had, and stirred a longing deep inside that he couldn't explain.

It had been an interesting experience, like riding a raft down a rushing river without a paddle. But each time they peeked at him through the glass panes or smiled and waved, he felt an odd tugging in the center of his chest, like stretching an unused muscle. It hurt, but felt good at the same time.

Closing his laptop, he took his glass out onto the

front porch. Beaux trotted alongside. The streetlights had blinked on, casting their yellow glow across the front lawn. He liked the stillness of evening and the solitude of the darkness. It gave him time to reflect on things and organize his mind for the next day. Though lately all his thoughts centered on Lainie.

He needed to concentrate on the library. The job weighed on his mind every minute. Failure was not an option. Completing the job was his responsibility and he took his responsibilities seriously. He learned young that responsibility gave him a purpose and a direction. After his mother left, his dad had sought escape in drink to ease the emptiness. It had fallen to Shaw to take over the household until his dad was able to function again. Years later, after renewing his faith, Shaw had come to see his sense of responsibility as his gift. He'd use it to help, to fix, to smooth the way for others. He'd be the one people relied on, the go-to guy. He liked it that way. Clear. Direct. No complications.

He eased onto the porch swing, resting his drink on the arm, and set the swing in motion. His gaze drifted to Lainie's side of the house. A faint glow seeped from her front window. He fought an urge to knock on her door and ask her to join him.

As if reading his mind, Lainie stepped onto the porch, a small smile on her face.

"Mind if I join you?"

"Please." He scooted over to give her room on the swing.

She sat down and leaned back. "I've wanted to use this swing from the first moment I saw it."

"Why didn't you?"

"I didn't want to step over any boundaries."

His heart twisted. There would always be a boundary between them—the past—and nothing could change that. "There are no boundaries here, Lainie. You're welcome to explore any part of the house. You can even use my tools in the garage if you promise to put them back." She smiled at his attempt at humor, sending his heart racing. The pale light made her hair shimmer with each movement and he longed to run his fingers through the silken strands.

"Thanks. I really came out to give you an update on the library situation."

"Good news, I hope."

"Mostly. I received a call from Angie Durrant this afternoon. She said Blake found a way to allow me to work on the books at another location. She also said I could come on board as a consultant, which would give me access to the library computer system so I can start ordering the books we'll need. I would also be in charge of selecting all the furniture for the library."

"I told you they would come around."

"Well, the bad news is, while I'll be officially on the payroll as a consultant, I won't get a paycheck until my job is completed."

"So it's a good thing you're working for me. Now you can get started on the job you came here for."

"Yes, but it all hinges on finding a large enough space to work on the books. Do you have any suggestions?"

"Not off the top of my head, but I'll ask around and see what I can come up with."

"Thanks. I'd appreciate it." Lainie stared at her hands a moment as if gauging her next words. "The girls were disappointed they didn't get to see you tonight. They talked about you all day. They have declared you their favorite babysitter."

The compliment made him smile. "I'm sure they did. I caved to their every request."

"It's nice for them to have a male presence in their lives. They've been surrounded with women up until now."

Shaw swallowed. Was she asking him to step in and be that role model for the girls? Doubtful, but he couldn't dismiss the longing in the brown depths of her eyes. "Have you thought about getting married again? You're young, beautiful, with a lot of love to give the right man."

She looked away, her fingers clutching the chain holding up the swing. "No. Most guys I meet aren't interested in a woman with kids. The last man I dated told me a real man wouldn't want to raise some other guy's kids."

Shaw's fingers curled into fists. What kind of jerk would say something like that to Lainie? "He was wrong. You know that, don't you? A man who loved you would love your girls because they are part of you." Her brown eyes reflected tender gratitude, sending Shaw's pulse tripping.

Her voice was soft when she spoke. "What about you? Don't you ever think about settling down?"

Not until lately. He looked away. "Nope. I'm not the marrying kind."

"Is that why you only date a woman twice, so you can't get too close?"

"Who told you that? That's not true. I'm a busy guy. I don't have time to play around."

"Really? I thought maybe you were playing the old 'dump them before they can dump you' game."

Her observation pierced like an arrow into the center of his heart. She was wrong. He'd allowed his reputation with the ladies to stand because it prevented his dates from getting ideas. But he didn't dump his dates. He just never called them again. Shaw hid his emotion behind an "Are you kidding me?" expression. "You've been spending too much time in the psychology section of your library."

Lainie's eyes narrowed. "Maybe so." She shrugged. "Anyway, I had another reason for coming out here. I'm in need of your handyman skills again. One of the kitchen drawers is stuck."

Grateful for the diversion, Shaw stood. "Let's take a look at it."

In the kitchen, Lainie pointed to the half-opened drawer. "If it was any other one, I'd leave it alone, but we need silverware."

Shaw tugged on the sides, but the drawer refused to budge. "Can't have a family meal without knives and forks."

"So tell me about your family."

He was beginning to wish Lainie had never joined him on the porch. Her questions were far too probing for his liking. "My dad and me. That's it." He wiggled the drawer side to side.

"Your mom?"

Stooping, he examined the drawer slides, searching for the spot that was stuck, ignoring the sudden clenching in his stomach. "Walked out when I was twelve. Never saw her again." He stood, then grasped the sides with both hands, braced himself and yanked. Hard. The drawer broke free with a loud snap. Shaw set the broken drawer on the countertop, giving it the once-over again. "The slides are broken. I'll replace them, but for now, you'll have to use it like this."

"It's okay. I'll put the silverware someplace else."

He turned to face her and found her close at his side. She took his hand, squeezing it gently. "I'm so sorry. I know how it feels to lose a parent. My dad died when I was in high school. But I can't imagine losing your mother that way."

Shaw looked into her eyes, his heart beating wildly. His gaze caressed the soft lines of her face and the graceful curve of her neck. He inhaled the sweet strawberry scent that had lingered in his senses from the first moment he'd seen her at the police station. She stole his breath away. Her small hand fit perfectly in his. He wanted to hold it forever.

His cell phone dinged, breaking the spell. She released his hand, leaving him feeling lost and adrift. He took a shaky breath, trying to recover his composure and remember what they were talking about. Family. Right.

Lainie stepped back, brushing her hair behind her ear. "Thanks for looking at the drawer."

"Sure. Just set it on the porch after you've emptied it. I'll get to it as soon as I can."

"Okay."

"Good night."

Outside on the back porch, Shaw exhaled a pent-up breath. What had just happened between them? Lainie had taken his hand, and the connection between them had vibrated with awareness. He'd read compassion and understanding in her pretty eyes, giving him hope that maybe someday she'd be able to forgive him and they could be friends.

He entered his side of the house, chiding himself for creating fantasies. But maybe he could show his appreciation. Do something for her and the girls. Natalie had been disappointed there wasn't a swing in the backyard. That was something he could correct. And what better way to touch a mom's heart than by making her children happy?

Or gain her approval. He wanted that. He wanted Lainie to see beyond the past and erase the image she had of him. He wasn't that man anymore.

But he couldn't think of that now. They were under his protection, and until that obligation ended, he'd have to keep his emotional barriers in place.

He needed to remember that Lainie wasn't for him.

Lainie took a bite of her toast and tapped a few more keys on Shaw's computer. As soon as possible, she would buy one of her own. Having access to the internet and the information available was vital. Of course, once the library was up and running, she'd have use of that computer, but having one at home would be nice, too.

She closed her eyes and leaned back in the chair. Except, so far it hadn't been much help in finding a place to work on the library books. She'd run out of options. She'd called churches and civic groups, but none of them were willing to donate space. And the costs of renting available space were too high. She was beginning to think the whole idea was hopeless.

Being a stranger in town with few connections, and the person usurping the crown from the former librarian, didn't make things easier. If she were a native, she'd probably be home free. Of course, she was being a tad unrealistic. She'd gained approval from the board just yesterday afternoon, and it was only eight in the morning now.

"Mommy. There's a swing in the yard!" Giggles and

squeals accompanied the sound of little feet pounding down the stairs. Natalie ran to Lainie's side, her eyes bright with excitement.

Chrissy hurried to a stop beside her sister. "Two of them."

"What are you talking about?" Natalie dashed to the back door and pulled it open.

Chrissy tugged on her mother's hand, urging her up. "Come see."

"Hurry, Mommy."

She followed her daughters outside. Natalie hopped down the porch steps and ran across the grass. Chrissy held the handrail, moving as quickly as her little legs would allow. She smiled, pointing to the yard. "See, Mommy, I told you."

Lainie walked across the lawn to the old live oak tree at the back corner of the yard. One thick limb now anchored two swings, the perfect height from the ground for two children.

Chrissy joined her sister, clapping her hands with joy. "This one's mine."

A surge of gratitude and appreciation swelled Lainie's heart. She touched her fingers to her lips to still her emotions. Shaw had taken her daughter's wish to heart. She'd have to thank him for his thoughtful gesture.

"Push me, Mommy."

Stepping behind Natalie, Lainie gave a firm push, unable to keep from smiling. Her girls would spend hours out here. Shaw had no way of knowing that he'd also given her a gift. She'd dreamed of this for a long time. Beaux barked and loped up to join them.

With the girls captivated by the new swings, Lainie resumed her search for a place to set up her library work. Gwen had called, but had nothing to report, though she promised to keep looking.

The morning stretched on, and with each failed phone call, Lainie's discouragement increased. She had run out of ideas and enthusiasm. Having her plan to catalog the books approved meant nothing if she couldn't find a place to work. Sitting back in her chair, she rubbed her temples trying to ease a throbbing headache.

The familiar cheery whistle of the postman gave her an excuse to take a much-needed break. Lifting the mail from the box beside the front door, she sorted through the stack, letting out a small squeal when she saw an envelope from her bank. She squeezed the paper, feeling the plastic card inside. Finally. Her life was back in her control. Now she could give Shaw back his credit card and pay him for the cell phone.

Back in the kitchen, she glanced outside. The girls were still swinging. On their stomachs this time. She wanted to thank Shaw for his kindness. She picked up her phone, but hesitated. She never called him at work. She didn't want to do anything that would slow the progress on the library. She could go in person. A phone call wouldn't convey her sincere appreciation for the swings the way a face-to-face would. Plus, then she could return the credit card to him. It would be safer.

Of course, she could wait until he got home tonight, but he'd been working later and later. There was no telling when he'd get in. Probably long after she'd gone to bed. She glanced at the kitchen clock. Gwen was taking the kids to an animated feature this afternoon. That would be the perfect time to go see Shaw. And the library. It occurred to her that she'd never even seen her future workplace.

As soon as the girls left for the movie, Lainie changed into her aqua sundress and applied a little makeup before slipping into her sandals. The library was located a block off the square and she pulled to a stop across the street. The building wasn't at all what she had expected. When Shaw had told her about the old Webster house, she'd imagined a dark stone building, like something out of a gothic novel. But the Dover library was going to be housed in a stately, golden brick mansion. The two-story structure boasted an angular tower on one side with arched windows. Double wooden doors flanked by stone corbels welcomed visitors. Graceful windows on either side were topped with arched lintels, and an impressive parapet ran the length of the roof.

Seeing the building for the first time cemented her determination to make sure it was completed on schedule so she could work every day in this stunning home. She'd questioned coming to see Shaw in person, but now she was glad she had. She would ask him to let her peek inside. Her curiosity was on fire.

As she walked along the driveway, a wave of doubt formed in the back of her mind. Thanking Shaw in person had seemed like a good idea earlier. But now she found herself reluctant. Something had happened between them last night. She'd seen a different side to him when he'd told her about his mother. His vulnerability had touched her heart. She'd taken his hand, and the contact had short-circuited her pulse. She hadn't wanted to let go. What was wrong with her? She couldn't be attracted to Shaw McKinney. It was impossible. Out of the question. Not to mention, wrong.

So why was she here in person to see him? Why hadn't she waited for him to come home or called him on his cell or left him a note taped to a pane on the French door? She couldn't explain this strange compulsion to see him again. Which was ridiculous, because she lived in his house.

Lainie chewed on her bottom lip. She needed to be honest. He'd called her beautiful, and his words had touched something dormant deep inside her. The feminine part she'd denied for a long time. When Shaw looked at her with those intense blue eyes, she felt attractive and cherished. She missed feeling that way. But she shouldn't put too much stock in what he said. He was a man skilled at turning women's heads, making them feel special.

She stopped beside the building, glancing down at the flowing skirt on her sundress. Why had she changed clothes? Her shorts and T-shirt would have been perfectly appropriate to stop by to see Shaw. She should go home. She would hand him his credit card, say thanks for the swings and that would be that.

"Lainie. What are you doing here? Is everything all right?"

Caught. Lainie looked at Shaw, who had appeared from around the back of the building. His blue eyes were narrowed in concern, his stubble-darkened jaw rigid. A well-used leather tool belt hugged his lean hips over faded jeans. With the white hard hat, he looked like an ad for the well-dressed carpenter, and all male. Her mouth went dry. Had he asked her a question? She blinked. "Oh, yes. Everything is fine. I came by to return your card and to see the library."

Her cheeks warmed and her stomach did a funny twist. His dark, penetrating eyes punctured her last shreds of confidence. Coming here was a bad idea. A very bad idea.

She didn't want him to think she'd come here for him, because she hadn't. That would be unthinkable. Unforgivable. What she was feeling was a crazy mixture of gratitude and stress. Not attraction.

She forced a smile. She'd make this quick, then get back home.

Shaw studied Lainie closely. She was flushed and fidgety. Not at all like her normal self. He wasn't convinced she was all right. He took a step closer. She flinched and quickly opened her purse, pulling out the prepaid card he'd given her that first day, and handing it to him with a tight smile.

"My replacement cards came today so I won't need this one any longer. But thank you. I didn't use much of it."

He took the card reluctantly, hurt that she was so eager to return his gift. "I didn't intend for you to give this back. It was for emergencies."

"I know. But I can handle that myself now. And—" she bit her lip, grasping the strap on her shoulder bag with one hand "—I wanted say thank-you for putting up the swings for the girls. They found them this morning and refused to eat breakfast before playing on them." She held his gaze. "You made them both very happy."

Her sincere words touched him deeply, leaving him tongue-tied and searching for an appropriate reply. "I wasn't sure about how low to place the seats. I hope they were okay." Lainie smiled, her eyes turning a warm cocoa color and causing that wobbly sensation in his knees.

"They were both perfect."

Pride swelled inside his chest. Lainie's compliments made him feel like a hero. He'd made her happy. "Good. I'm glad they liked them." He enjoyed the sight of her standing in the sunlight, her eyes sparkling, a happy smile bringing a glow to her face.

She shifted her feet and looked past him to the building. "So this is going to be my new library. I love the architecture of this old home."

Aware he was staring, he looked over his shoulder, taking a second to compose himself. "Yeah. It's one of the oldest homes in Dover. Artemus Webster was a cotton baron and was influential in bringing the railroad through here." It occurred to him Lainie had never been inside the building. "Would you like a tour?"

"I'd love that. I haven't had much time to think about what the library would look like. I'm too busy just trying to start work."

"Wait here. I'll be right back." Shaw quickly retrieved a hard hat from his truck and handed it to her. She frowned.

"Do I have to?"

"I'm afraid so. This is a government job, which makes it mandatory."

She grimaced, but put the hat on. It slid down to her ears. Shaw adjusted the inner webbing to make it smaller, then took her arm and guided her back to the front along the sidewalk leading to the recently restored double cypress entry doors. He wanted her first impression to be memorable.

"How's the search going?"

Lainie grimaced. "Terrible. I don't think there's anyplace in Dover I can use. No one wants to donate space, and the cost of renting is too high."

"Don't give up hope. I've still got a few places to check into."

Shaw was glad the exterior was completed. He doubted Lainie would have been impressed with the run-down state of the old home when he had first started the restoration. The beige brick facade had been cleaned and repainted, new windows installed in the bay wall, broken parapets restored and new sidewalks poured. All that remained was the landscaping.

Pulling open the doors, he waited for Lainie to enter, but kept close enough so he could see her reaction. The foyer of the old house was paneled in cherrywood, with marble floors and the original gas chandelier rewired for electricity. Ahead, the intricately carved staircase rose to the second floor. Lainie's slow intake of breath told him she was suitably impressed.

"This is gorgeous."

"It took a lot of restoration work, but I think I got it pretty close to the original."

"You did this?" She ran her hand along the burled wood insets on the walls.

"I did." Was she impressed? He wanted her to be. But then he realized his ego was getting out of hand and squelched the thought.

They stepped into the area that would become the lobby and Lainie's enthusiasm faded. Shaw felt a need to explain. "Over here will be your checkout counter. Jeb is building it at my shop. Behind it is your office and rooms for meetings or classes. The rest of this floor will be bookshelves. These wood floors will be refinished."

He led her to the other side of the building where the wall bayed out creating a cozy nook for reading.

"This is where the donor's collection will be kept. It'll be carpeted."

Lainie moved around the area, her expression troubled. Shaw watched her closely as they toured the second floor and the area that would house the computer center. He'd seen this reaction many times before when showing an unfinished space to a client. Some people could easily envision the end result, while others, like Lainie, weren't able to see beyond the bare walls and construction debris. They exited through the back entrance. Shaw held his breath, bracing for Lainie's reaction.

She returned the hard hat, staring back at the old house and chewing her bottom lip. "It's so empty, and there's so much work to do. Are you sure you can finish it before the deadline in three weeks?"

"I think so. I know it doesn't look like it, but we're in the final stages. You'll be surprised how quickly it'll all come together."

"I hope so." Her gaze scanned the area. "Shaw, what's that building?"

He looked in the direction she was pointing. "That's the old carriage house."

"Does it belong to the library?"

"Yes. But it's not part of the construction. It'll be closed up and kept for future use. Why?"

"It looks like a large space."

"About the size of a three-car garage."

"Can I see inside?"

"Sure." He wasn't sure why she was interested. Shaw unlocked the door and stepped inside. The yellow brick building was a cluttered mess of boxes, old tools and discarded furniture. "Like I said, it's not much."

Lainie stepped farther into the space. "It's perfect."

She smiled at him, the enthusiasm back in her eyes. "Why can't I work on the library books here?"

Shaw took a look around. The space was good. "I suppose it would work. But it needs to be cleaned out." He scanned the ceiling, warming to the idea. "I could install a couple of small air-conditioning units to cool the room. There's already Wi-Fi active in the library so you could set up your computer. But I don't have any crew to spare."

"Maybe we can find some volunteers."

Volunteers. He smiled and nodded. "I think I know the perfect ones to recruit. My woodworking students. They can clear this out in a day." The excitement in her eyes swelled his chest. He knew in that moment he'd do anything to make her happy.

Lainie fisted her hands in triumph. "This will be perfect. Once the windows are cleaned and this stuff out of the way, we'll have more than enough room, and when it comes time to move the books, they'll be right here. And it won't cost us anything." She clasped her hands together. "You won't charge us, will you?"

He had to laugh at her worried expression. "Of course not. Besides, that would be up to the library board, and I don't see them charging themselves."

"I was beginning to think I'd never find a place. And to think it was right here all along."

Lainie's joy washed through him like sunshine, casting warmth and light into parts of himself he'd forgotten existed. Her delight drew him like nothing else ever had.

She faced him, her bright smile still in full force. "This is going to solve all my problems. I'll never be able to thank you for this." She flung her arms around his neck in a quick hug.

Shaw tentatively slipped his arms around her back, his senses on overload, his heart pounding. "It was your idea."

Slowly, she drew back, her hands sliding down the front of his shirt, as if reluctant to let go. Her gaze locked with his. Her eyes were wide and filled with surprise, but there was a question there, as well. His attention moved to her slightly parted lips. If he moved a mere inch, lowered his head a fraction, he could kiss the lips he'd thought about every night since she'd come to Dover. He looked at her and realized she was thinking the same thing.

Abruptly, she stepped back, her face pale. "I'm sorry. I mean, I shouldn't have done that. It was—"

He wouldn't let her feel badly about what had happened. "It was a hug between friends. That's all." He read gratitude in her big brown eyes. "You better get busy. Call Angie and tell her I said the carriage house is available. I'll call the boys and get them started."

"Okay." She started out, but stopped and threw a smile over her shoulder, leaving him dazed like a schoolboy and unable to move long after she'd disappeared. If he had any sense, he'd keep his distance from his lovely tenant. His feelings were growing, and that could only lead to a painful outcome. He didn't need any more of that in his life. Pulling out his cell, he started making calls. He had to remember there was a big line drawn in the sand between them. Crossing it would have serious consequences for everyone.

Chapter Seven

Saturday morning Lainie drove to the library filled with happy expectations. Today she would finally start cataloging the books from the donor's private collection. Since discovering the carriage house a couple of days ago, things had moved swiftly. Angie Durrant had approved the carriage house as a suitable working area, and by the end of Friday, Lainie had been hired as consultant, signed contracts, gained access to the library system and been given all the information she needed to begin ordering books and furniture for the library. The books from the collection had been delivered to the carriage house this morning, and she was eager to get started. Gwen had agreed to watch the girls whenever she was needed. It was amazing how things could change in one week.

Parking her car beside the carriage house, she couldn't keep memories of being in Shaw's arms from resurfacing despite her willing them not to. A rush of hot embarrassment rose up her neck. She'd acted impulsively the other day, out of gratitude and excitement. He'd been gracious and brushed the hug off as a simple friendly gesture. But she knew the truth. She was attracted to Shaw, shameful as that was. And she had no explanation at all for her unexpected desire to kiss him. Each day it became harder to match her old assumptions about him to the reality of him. He wasn't arrogant and selfish. He was confident and thoughtful. She tried repeatedly to shove him back into the old mold, but he kept breaking out in new and surprising ways.

He'd come home early the other night, and she'd watched him walk to the swings. He pushed the girls for a long time before going inside. The sight had touched her heart. She'd seen his affection for her children, and they adored him. Shaw fit so easily into their lives. But she didn't want him to. Sighing, she faced a truth she'd been avoiding. Her feelings for him were changing. Somewhere, he'd stopped being the enemy and become a friend.

But she had to remember Shaw was a charmer, a man who won women's hearts with little more than a glance. She couldn't read anything more into his attention than what it was—his obligation to her and the girls because of the past.

She was so confused emotionally that she was starting to lose sleep at the time she needed it most. Shoving thoughts of Shaw aside, she got out of the car. Since arriving in Dover, she'd felt adrift, without a solid footing to stand on. Working on the collection would keep her mind off her conflicted feelings and provide the structure and control she needed.

Lainie stepped inside the carriage house and into a wall of boxes blocking her way. Puzzled, she moved to the worktable and picked up the delivery notice. The donor's private library consisted of three thousand titles.

She'd anticipated a few hundred not a few thousand. This was a much bigger job than she'd ever imagined. Why hadn't she asked about the amount sooner? Glancing back at the mountain of boxes, her heart sank. Even working around the clock, she doubted she could finish cataloging in time for the library to open. She'd given her word. But there was no way she could do this alone. She would need help.

But who? Other than Shaw and Gwen, she didn't know anyone in town, and neither of them could set aside their own lives to help her. She needed someone with experience, someone who could step in and start work without needing any training. Someone like... Millie.

She would be the perfect person to ask. She had the experience and intimate knowledge of the town and their reading preferences. Plus a love of the library. But she would never agree to work with the person she believed stole her position.

Still, Lainie had to try. She didn't like being a divisive element in her new town. Reaching out to Millie in a gesture of peace and friendship might be a way to smooth the troubled waters.

She mulled the idea over the rest of the day, and by Sunday morning she'd formulated a plan. When she arrived at Peace Community Church, her hopes were rising. She would talk to Millie at the monthly luncheon in the fellowship hall after the service. It would be the perfect place. A relaxed environment surrounded by lots of people.

But as she and the girls were finishing their meals, Lainie was beginning to think her plan was futile. She hadn't seen Millie anywhere at the luncheon. As the girls went off to play with their new friends, Lainie scanned the room once again. She'd never met Millie, but Gwen had pointed her out before the service. The prospect of approaching the woman sent butterflies aloft in Lainie's stomach. She'd almost given up hope when she spotted the stately former librarian standing near the back door of the hall. Gathering her courage, Lainie rose, trying to ignore her sweating palms and the tightness in her throat. *Please Lord, open her heart and let her see the benefit of working with me.*

"Excuse me, Mrs. Tedrow." Millie turned around, a deep scowl on her narrow face. "I'm Lainie Hollings."

"I know who you are."

Lainie struggled to ignore the cold tone in the woman's voice and proceed. "I've started cataloging the books our library benefactor donated, but it's a massive job. I'll admit that it's more work than I can do on my own. If the new facility is to open on time and meet the requirements of the donation, I'll need help getting them into the system. There's also the matter of all the new books that must be ordered." She took a deep breath, looking for a softening in Millie's glare, but finding none. "With your extensive knowledge and experience with the library, I thought perhaps you'd like to help me get things organized."

"You want me to be your assistant?" Millie's lips pressed together tightly. "Of all the nerve."

"It's for the good of the town. I'm sure you want the library to open on time as much as I do. You know the reading tastes of the people here, and I don't. I want to make sure the books we offer encompass the interests of all the residents."

Millie raised her chin, looking down her nose. "You

can figure that out yourself. In time. Now, if you'll excuse me, I don't believe we have anything else to say to one another."

Lainie fought to control the feelings of humiliation and disappointment. Natalie came to her side, her little face set in an angry scowl.

"I don't like you. You're mean to my mommy."

Millie stopped, squared her shoulders and turned around.

Horrified, Lainie pulled her arm around her daughter. "Natalie, apologize to Mrs. Tedrow at once."

"I don't want to."

Millie looked at Natalie. "Perhaps your father should instruct you on the proper manner in which to address your elders."

Natalie leaned back against Lainie, her anger fading. "I don't have a father. He's in heaven with Jesus."

Lainie swallowed a lump of sadness mingled with regret. "I'm sorry, Mrs. Tedrow. I won't bother you again." Wrapping an arm around her child's shoulders, she started back to her table. She sensed all eyes in the room were on them, but a quick look around proved that notion false. She scanned the room for Shaw. She could use a friend right now. She had seen little of him since she'd started working in the carriage house. She had the feeling he was avoiding her.

She'd been convinced of that when she'd arrived at church this morning in time to see Shaw embrace a petite blonde woman. She'd held his face in her hands, her smile revealing her affection for him. They'd walked into the church together arm in arm. She'd seen them seated closely in a pew near the front.

Apparently, she'd been hasty in thinking he didn't

fit the image she'd had of him. He was easily distracted by the next pretty face. Not that it mattered to her. She had no reason to believe that Shaw was attracted to her. A mother of two wasn't his type. While she might find him attractive, she could never have romantic feelings for him. "Natalie, go get your sister. She's playing in the corner with her friends."

"Lainie, is everything all right? I saw you talking to Millie."

Shaw appeared behind her. Where had he come from? "I'm fine. I asked Millie to help me with the books, but she refused."

"I can't say I'm surprised." He touched her elbow. "If you have a moment, I'd like you to meet some friends of mine."

He steered her toward the pretty blonde woman he'd sat with. He wanted to introduce her to his girlfriend? No way. She stopped. "I need to get home."

"Please. It'll only take a moment and they're anxious to meet you."

They? Did he have a fan club of females? Probably. Too tired and discouraged to argue, she followed him to a table on the other side of the room. The three women had been joined by a fourth whom Lainie recognized as Angie Durrant.

Shaw stopped beside the blonde seated next to Angie. "Ladies, I'd like you to meet our new head librarian, Lainie Hollings. Lainie, you know Angie. This is her daughter, Laura Holbrook, my former boss."

Lainie noticed the resemblance now between the blonde and Angie. "Nice to meet you." Shaw introduced the elegant and very pregnant dark-haired woman as Shelby Durrant, and the auburn-haired woman with the sweet smile as Ginger Durrant.

"We're so glad to meet you." Laura smiled warmly. "Mom has talked about you a lot. All good."

"She's going to be a tremendous asset to Dover." Angie glanced at Shaw with a motherly smile. "Since Shaw's become a businessman, we hardly see him. We demanded he sit with us today since all our men are on a Handy Works project."

"What's that?" Lainie asked.

Shaw explained. "That's the ministry the Durrants started to help with repairs for those who can't afford to hire the work done."

"What a wonderful idea."

Ginger smiled. "They will recruit you once you're settled."

"And I'll be more than happy to participate."

They chatted a few moments, then Lainie said goodbye. She'd been unduly relieved that the lovely women Shaw had been seated with were the Durrants—the happily married Durrants. That explained the warm hug from Laura Holbrook. She was his former boss. Of course they would be close. Kissing cousins close.

Shaw was not her problem. Millie was, and their encounter had been a disaster. She couldn't complete the book job in time without Millie's help. With the added task of selecting and ordering the furniture for the library, her time was stretched to the limit. She was grateful, but she worried that she might fall behind on her responsibilities.

Lainie had barely changed out of her church clothes and gone downstairs when Gwen knocked at the back door.

"I heard what that old sourpuss said to you. I knew

I should have stayed for the luncheon." She frowned as she took the glass of sweet tea Lainie offered. "My mother is behind this."

"What makes you say that?"

"Oh, Mom and Millie have been friends and neighbors since forever. They see any change as a bad thing. When the choir director decided to forgo robes, they had a fit. When the pastor was given an additional week of vacation, they were furious. They think he should be on call 24/7, three hundred and sixty-five. It's ridiculous."

"I hope I can find someone else to help me. If not, you may be watching my kids round the clock."

"I don't mind a bit. They are darlings. But don't give up yet." Gwen patted her arm and grinned. "I may be able to fix this for you. This attitude of theirs has been coming to a head for a while, and a talk with my mother is long overdue. Hang in there."

Lainie had no idea what Gwen was planning, but she hoped it would work. Getting the library stocked and ready was more overwhelming than she'd anticipated, and she was beginning to doubt her capabilities.

What if she failed to finish her job on time? The townspeople would really dislike her then. She'd be forced to leave Dover and start life over—again. All she wanted was to be settled once and for all. Why was that so difficult?

Shaw had scheduled the delivery of the cabinetry and counters for early Monday morning. He'd gone by the shop to make sure everything was ready. Jeb had pulled the large truck to a stop at the rear of the library right on time. If only all his subcontractors were as dependable.

They tackled the large reception counter first, which

was refusing to fit in the space. Shaw shoved his end of the eight-foot-long unfinished counter into place. Russ manhandled the other until the cabinet fit perfectly. "Looks good." Shaw stepped back and eyed the custom-designed piece of furniture that would be the checkout counter for the library.

Russ nodded, running a hand along the smooth wood. "Jeb did a good job. It's going to be mighty pretty when it's stained and sealed. I think Miss Lainie will be pleased."

Shaw glanced at his friend, seeing the teasing glint in the man's dark eyes. Had Russ picked up on his attraction to Lainie? He'd have to do a better job of keeping his feelings hidden.

"She'll be pleased when the place is done and she can go to work." Russ chuckled and went out to help Jeb bring in more cabinetry.

Shaw surveyed the large main room. Once all the cabinetry was installed, he could start on the baseboard and shoe mold, and if he could juggle the painting and staining crew with the floor refinishers, he could make up a couple days of work.

He'd been working full out for the past few days, and it was paying off. But it was costing him in other ways. He was getting home so late he hadn't seen Natalie and Chrissy. He missed them. He missed Lainie. He shouldn't, but he did. He'd only seen them once since the church lunch. Shaw wished he'd seen her talking to Millie sooner. He could have run interference for her, but he'd been trying to maintain a safe zone between them. When Laura had asked him to sit with her, he had jumped at the chance. He'd been thinking only about himself. He was supposed to be taking care of Lainie.

Even though Lainie was mere yards away in the carriage house, he'd deliberately avoided wandering back there to see her. The memory of her impulsive hug, the feel of her arms around him had lingered in his thoughts ever since. But it had also set off warning sirens he couldn't ignore. He was becoming too entangled in her life, too preoccupied with thoughts of her. It was a dangerous path for both of them. Time to pull back before someone got the wrong idea and ended up hurt. There was no room or time in his life right now for romance of any kind. He needed to focus his energy on getting the library finished. That was his main objective. Along with making sure Lainie and the girls were taken care of until then. Nothing more.

Outside, Shaw started toward the panel truck that held the cabinetry. A small car pulled along the drive and parked near the carriage house. He couldn't believe his eyes when he saw Millie Tedrow get out and go inside.

Remembering her rudeness to Lainie last Sunday, Shaw's protective instincts roared to life. He would not let the woman bully Lainie again. Just to be on the safe side, he'd make his presence known. Let the older woman know the new librarian had backup.

The carriage house door was open and he could hear voices from inside. The women were speaking quietly. No signs of an argument. Maybe he'd hang back a few moments to make sure. He stopped a few feet from the door, but the voices were clearly discernible, and he couldn't believe what he was hearing. Millie was apologizing.

"When I learned you were a widow raising your children alone, it made me look at things differently. I was widowed young, too, and had to raise my boys without a father. I know the struggles you face." She grimaced.

"And, Gwen gave her mother and me a good scolding. I'm ashamed of my behavior, Lainie. You reached out in love, and I smacked your hand away because my ego was bruised. Are you familiar with the passage in the Bible that talks about removing the log in your own eye before attempting to remove the speck in another's?"

Shaw heard Lainie reply softly that she was. It occurred to him that he was eavesdropping, but if he moved, he risked disturbing the women, and this was a crucial conversation. He'd ask forgiveness later. Millie spoke again.

"I think we all have logs in our eyes— things we see so clearly in others that we're oblivious to in ourselves. We think we've dealt with our pains and losses. We tell ourselves we've forgiven others and moved on. When my husband died, I was so angry. I threw myself into my job at the library to keep from feeling. Later, when my boys were grown, my work at the library was all I had. It gave me a respected position in town. I enjoyed the attention and the prestige. I didn't realize how my ego had gotten tied up in that title until I learned about you being the new librarian. I was upset. I felt you'd stolen something from me. But you didn't. I hope you can forgive me. And if the offer is still open, I'd be proud to work with you."

"Oh, Millie, of course I forgive you."

Shaw quietly moved back to his truck, marveling at Lainie's way with people. She could win anyone over, given the opportunity, and she did it with love and compassion. She had a warm heart and the ability to forgive.

Except where he was concerned.

Resting his forearms along the side of his truck bed, he faced the truth. He couldn't stay away from Lainie. His heart was reaching for her. His every thought, every

moment near her, increased the invisible thread bind-
ing him to her. He needed to rein in his emotions. His
only goal was to make things easy for Lainie until the
library was done.

"Shaw."

He looked up as Lainie hurried toward him across
the lawn. The sun reflected off her hair, the strands
swaying around her shoulders. "Hey."

"You won't believe what just happened. Millie has
agreed to come to work with me. With the two of us,
we should be able to finish everything by the deadline."

"That's great. It's about time something started going
right."

She nodded. "She'll be back this afternoon to get
started."

Shaw told himself to maintain some control, but her
smile was too much to resist. He touched the side of her
cheek, awed at the softness. "I'm glad, Lainie. I told you
people would come around, didn't I?"

"You did." Her smile faded and she took a step back.
"I'd better get to work. I, uh, just wanted to let you know
the good news."

Shaw watched her walk away, more determined than
ever to strengthen the walls around his emotions. For
his own protection. Whenever she was near, he lost all
common sense and reason. Lainie was off-limits.

He had his future planned out for the next five years.
Starting with finishing the library on time. Then he had
to get his business on solid ground. He had people depending on him—Russ, Jeb and the eight other guys
who worked for him. There was no room in his life for
the domestic scene.

So why couldn't he stop thinking about a family of

his own? He'd always been comfortable being alone. Getting too attached to people usually ended in pain. Sooner or later, they would walk away. Like his mother. Like his former fiancée, Vicki. The only people he'd allowed to get close were Russ and Laura Durrant. Even with them, he'd kept a part of himself private.

Logically, he knew his mom didn't walk out because of him. His father had been open about their marital struggles, but Vicki's rejection was another matter. That was all him. She'd walked away because he'd been unable to give her what she wanted. His whole heart. He'd come to the conclusion that he wasn't cut out for a long-term relationship. Maybe Vicki was right and he didn't know how to give his heart to anyone.

Instead, he'd give his heart to his work. That was something he understood.

The carriage house was quiet. Millie was attending her Thursday morning Bible study. She'd wanted to stay and work, but Lainie had encouraged her to attend. They'd been working on the collection for a couple of days and had made significant progress, renewing Lainie's hopes of finishing on time. Millie was a godsend. They had drawn closer through their love of books and their experiences as widows raising young children. Together, they had chosen furniture for the library and started placing orders for the body of books that would fill the shelves. Some of the orders wouldn't arrive in time for the opening, but the majority would.

The carriage house walls suddenly pressed in on her. She'd been working hard all morning. She needed a break and some fresh air. The weather this week was

pleasant for a Mississippi June. A cool front had come
through bringing a brief respite from the rising humidity.

Curious about the progress being made in the library, Lainie strolled across the grass toward the back
door where Shaw's truck was parked. In a few days, the
lovely lawn would be graded and an asphalt parking lot
installed. She understood the need, but the thought of
losing a beautiful lawn made her sad.

As she neared the truck, a man emerged, moving
quickly. She remembered his name was Thad Comier,
a friendly, pleasant man with a soft Cajun accent she'd
met a few days ago. But the look on Thad's face now
was one of anger. Shaw followed him. She stopped,
surprised by the fierce look on his face.

"I'm not interested in your comfort, Thad." They
stopped beside Shaw's truck. He reached into the back
of the bed, pulled out a pair of clear safety glasses and
handed them to Thad. "You will wear these or you'll
not work for me. Is that clear?"

Thad muttered a response Lainie couldn't make out.

"Then go buy yourself some of the high-end kind
that you *can* see through. I need all hands on this job,
and we don't have time to take you to hospital because
you're injured. *To konprann?*"

Thad stared at Shaw a moment before responding.
"Yeah. I understand." Grabbing the glasses, he stomped
back inside.

Shaw looked up and saw her, his expression softening. "How's it going?" He approached her with a slow,
easy gait.

Lainie glanced past him in the direction of the library. "What was that all about?"

Shaw shrugged. "Thad doesn't like the way things

look through the safety glasses. He claims he can't see to do his job."

"Is that true?"

"Maybe. But none of the other guys have trouble. He doesn't understand the need for many of the safety precautions I take. Some guys like to think they're daredevils and don't need to follow rules. If Thad doesn't shape up, I'll have to let him go. I can't have his reckless attitude infecting the others."

Anger erupted in her chest. "So you're a big safety advocate now?" She didn't even try to keep the sarcasm out of her voice. "Where was that concern five years ago? Or did you develop this big commitment as a way to deal with your guilt?" Grief tightened her throat making it impossible to say any more. She spun around and stormed back to the carriage house. She wanted to cry, but there were no tears, only anger. And a need to understand. Maybe if Shaw had been as aware then as he appeared to be now, her life would be different today.

It was his fault she was alone, his fault that her girls would never know their father.

Inside the carriage house, she sank into a chair, cradling her head in her hands. She felt a thousand years old. She was tired of being sad, of being angry. Tired of asking why and trying to make sense of the past.

Shaw, the big safety advocate. Everyone was so impressed. It didn't matter how cautious he was now. He hadn't been when it really mattered. No amount of precaution, or adherence to the rules, could wash away the one time he'd failed.

She'd been distracted by his charm, his helpful attitude. She'd let herself forget who he was and what he'd let happen.

She wouldn't make that mistake again.

Shaw stopped at the carriage house door, his hand lingering on the handle. He didn't want to have this confrontation, but he couldn't go on like this. It was time they dealt with the past.

He stepped inside, searching out Lainie. She stood near the worktable, back stiff, arms crossed defensively across her chest. She didn't turn around when he approached. He took a deep breath. "Maybe it's time we got this out in the open. I'm tired of dancing around the elephant in the room."

She whirled and faced him. "You were supposed to watch out for him, make sure he was safe. He should have been secured to that roof." Tears welled up in her eyes and spilled down her cheeks.

He resisted the urge to pull her close and comfort her. "He was. That was a twelve-twelve pitch roof. We all had to use toe boards and harnesses. I made sure he had his on correctly."

"You should have checked again."

"You're right. I should have. I've been over it a thousand times in my head. Wondering what else I could have done. What I missed. Lainie, if I could go back and change it, I would. You have to believe that." Shaw ran a hand through his hair. "I'd checked his harness several times that morning, but each time, he'd loosened it again. He said he didn't like the way the harness felt. I warned him again to keep it pulled tight, then I went back to work on my section. The next thing I knew—" Lainie's weeping was tearing him apart, but he continued. "He had the ability to become a decent carpenter, but he would lose focus, and when he didn't understand something, he'd get angry. That's why Mr. Beaumont was going to let him go at the end of the week."

Inwardly, Shaw kicked himself for letting that fact slip out. It would only hurt Lainie more.

"You were going to fire him?"

The shock in her brown eyes told him she wouldn't be satisfied until she knew it all. "He was reckless and he had a bad attitude. It was starting to affect the other men. I couldn't keep him on."

She placed a hand over her mouth, her dark eyes filled with sorrow. She moved away, raking her hands along her scalp before hugging her arms across her middle. "I never got to tell him our good news. He never knew we were going to have Chrissy. I was going to tell him that night."

Shaw's gut kicked. Would this pain and guilt never end? He turned away, unable to bear the sight of her in pain. Her sadness wrenched his heart. He wanted to hold her and ease her sorrow, but he knew she wouldn't welcome it. There was nothing more he could say. "I can never make up to you for what happened. And I don't expect you to forgive me. But for what it's worth, that day changed my life forever, too." He opened the door and walked out.

His heart hurt for Lainie, but finally talking to her about that day had cleared away the cobwebs from his mind. He *had* done all he could to protect Hollings. He'd checked the man's harness numerous times. He'd warned him he could lose his job. He'd warned him of the dangers, but Hollings had refused to listen.

Those facts had been buried beneath Shaw's pain over the death of a man under his care. But talking to

Lainie, saying the words aloud, had clarified the events. Shaw stopped near the back of his truck, resting his hands on his hips. A sense of freedom, of release, had taken root inside. He wasn't at fault. He didn't need to blame himself or feel guilty anymore. He'd asked the Lord to forgive him, and he was confident He had. But Shaw had been unable to forgive himself. Until now. Maybe now he could begin to.

A gentle hand touched his shoulder. "Everything okay, fella?"

Shaw gave Russ a smile over his shoulder. "Yeah. Actually, I think they finally are."

Russ nodded at the carriage house. "Something happen in there?"

"We cleared the air. I told her what happened that day, and it made me realize what you've always tried to tell me. It wasn't my fault. I did everything I could. I couldn't force Hollings to obey the rules."

"He made his own choice that day. She'll come to see that herself eventually."

"I don't know. But I've let it go. I'm not going to think about it anymore."

"What about her? How are you going to stop thinking about her?"

That was a very good question, and Shaw prayed he had the inner strength to accomplish it. The best way was to stay at work. It's where he needed to focus anyway. Everyone lost if the library wasn't finished on time. That's what mattered. Not his feelings, or his heart, or his dreams.

He may no longer blame himself for the accident, but that didn't absolve him of his duty to Lainie. He wasn't at fault, but she was still his responsibility.

Chapter Eight

Lainie shoved her half-eaten sandwich into the brown bag, crumpled it and tossed it into the trash. Her lunch had tasted like dry paper. She loved egg salad, but she was too upset to eat. The confrontation with Shaw this morning had left her agitated and irritable. She'd waited years to confront him, to demand answers, to find some reason for the accident. But now that the moment had arrived, it didn't feel the way she had thought it would. She'd expected a sense of closure. Even validation that he was at fault.

Instead, she'd been forced to look at things from a different perspective. Was it possible that Craig was more at fault than Shaw? No. Impossible. That would change everything she'd thought about her husband and everything she'd believed for the past five years.

Search me, God, and know my heart; test me and know my anxious thoughts.

She buried her fingers in her hair. It was time to face the truth. Her husband had never liked taking orders or following advice. He'd fallen because he wanted to do things his way, not the right or safe way. Shaw had done all he could.

Learning that her husband was going to be let go wasn't a huge surprise, either. He'd become increasingly unhappy, directing most of his anger at Shaw. It wasn't the first time he'd lost a job because of his attitude. She simply hadn't wanted to believe he was that kind of man.

"Lainie, are you all right?"

She'd been so deep in thought she hadn't heard the car pull up or Millie enter the carriage house. "Fine." She tried to smile but felt sure her attempt was a failure. "I have some personal things to work out, that's all."

Millie laid her purse on the worktable, peering at her more closely. "Something happened while I was gone. What was it?"

In the short time Lainie had worked with the former librarian, she'd learned it was impossible to hide anything from her. "Shaw and I had a talk about the past."

"You mean the accident?"

Lainie jerked her head up. "You know about that?"

"I know enough. I'm good friends with Viola Franklin, Russ's wife. She gave me the CliffsNotes version." She pulled up a folding chair and sat. "Do you feel better now that you've both spoke your piece?"

"No. Truth is I'm not sure how I feel."

"I'm not surprised. It's comforting to have someone to blame. It helps us make sense of things. My husband died of an aggressive form of cancer. For years, I blamed the doctors for not doing more, for not catching the disease sooner. Then one day, I read a verse in the Bible. 'In the world you will have trouble. But take heart! I have overcome the world.' I had to finally accept that illness is a fact of life. So are accidents."

"Shaw said that day changed his life." Lainie frowned, trying to understand. "How? He went on with his carefree bachelor life. He started his own business. I was left to raise my daughters alone."

Millie patted Lainie's arm. "When we're hurting, all we can see is our side. We forget that there's always two sides to everything. From what Viola told me, Shaw was a broken man back then. He'd lost his faith in himself and his God. One thing I've learned in my sixty-plus years on this old earth is that everything we do affects other people. Our choices and our decisions are like ripples on the pond. They go out and change things whether we realize it or not."

Millie's wisdom and Shaw's comments churned in the back of Lainie's mind the rest of the day. She'd never considered how the accident had affected Shaw. She hadn't wanted to. But now she could think of nothing else. A man had died on his watch. He would have felt guilty. Horribly so. A broken man. Was that the pain she'd seen behind his eyes sometimes?

She'd started to remember things about her husband. Things she'd forgotten. He was impatient, and he liked to break the rules and challenge authority when he didn't see a reason for something. He carried a grudge far too long.

"Mommy, what was Daddy's superpower?"

Natalie's question pulled her thoughts back to bedtime and getting her girls settled for the night. Lainie sat on the edge of the bed, brushing hair off her daughter's forehead. "What do you mean?"

Chrissy's blue eyes blinked. "You said he was a superhero, and they have cool powers. What was his?"

Powers? Did her children believe that? She'd always tried to speak about their father in positive, glowing terms. They would have no memory of him, so she wanted them to think of him as a father they could be proud of as they grew up. But maybe, in her zeal, she'd given them an unrealistic picture. Craig was a good dad and husband, and he had loved them, but he had his faults like everyone else.

She looked into Chrissy's questioning eyes. Pulling the covers up, she stroked each soft cheek in turn. "He didn't have powers, sweetie. But he loved us, and that's a special kind of power. Your father loved us very much. That's all you need to remember."

As she prepared for bed, she realized that in accepting Craig's part in the accident, her own burden had eased. Facing the truth, letting go of the blame, had brought an unexpected feeling of freedom and release. Blame was a heavy burden. There'd been no reason to blame Shaw. Her anger should have been directed at Craig for not being careful, for not thinking about what could happen if he refused to take safety precautions.

A broken man. She'd wondered why the Lord had brought Shaw back into her life. Maybe it was so she could finally face the truth and be freed from the past.

Tugging up the covers, she closed her eyes and set the day's events aside. But one image refused to fade— the look of pain and guilt in Shaw's eyes when she had told him Craig had never learned about her pregnancy. He'd looked wounded to his soul, as if she'd sliced his heart in two.

Shaw was a man who took his responsibilities to

heart. But he wasn't responsible for this, and it was time she told him so, and let him know she no longer blamed him.

As she drifted off to sleep, another thought floated in her mind. In accepting that Craig had been at fault for the fall, she'd closed the door on her past, but opened a door to the future—one she'd been afraid to face.

She was falling in love with Shaw McKinney. What kind of woman did that make her? Guilty or not, Shaw was at the heart of her loss. Shouldn't she be more respectful of her husband's memory? When was it okay to let go and move on?

That question floated through her dreams all night.

The clank and grind of the outdated air-conditioning system kicked on, sending welcome cool air into the old kitchen. The pleasant temperatures of the past few days had been replaced by highs in the upper nineties. Even now in the late evening, the humidity still thickened the air.

The distinctive rumble of Shaw's truck drew Lainie's glance to the wall clock. Nine-fifteen. He'd worked late again. If this library ever opened, they'd both have to take a long vacation to recuperate. Not together, of course. Laying aside the dish towel, she went to the back door. She needed to talk to him as soon as possible to let him know she no longer blamed him. She'd gone over her speech a dozen times, but it always came out sounding insincere, or worse yet, condescending. She'd finally decided to take the first opportunity that came her way and asked the Lord to provide the words.

She heard the gate snap shut, and his tall frame walked toward the house. She stepped quietly onto the porch, never taking her eyes from him. His broad shoulders were sloped downward, and his stride lacked its usual confident lift. A wave of sympathy touched her. He was working hard to make the deadline. Just as she was. It meant so much to both of them. Shaw was a man of determination and commitment. He never backed down once he made up his mind. If he ever gave his heart to someone, it would be with the same devotion.

He glanced up, one corner of his mouth lifting when he saw her.

"Tough day?"

He stopped on the step below her, putting their faces on the same level and sending her heart bouncing. She was beginning to care a great deal for this man. It was foolish, but her heart refused to pull away. She'd been caught in his web of attraction like all the others before. Where was her pride?

"Tough, but productive. If we keep this up, we'll be finished ahead of time. I never thought I'd be able to say that." He stepped up beside her, now looking down at her with midnight-blue eyes.

Even in the faint glow of the porch light, she could see the tenderness in his gaze. She also saw something else. "Your arm. What happened?" She took his wrist in her hand, staring at the ugly five-inch scratch along his forearm. The blood had dried to a dark brown. Her stomach tightened at the thought of his being injured.

He shrugged. "Hard telling. Probably caught it on a nail or a piece of lumber. It's nothing. It happens all the time."

Lainie glared and tugged him into her kitchen. "It needs to be taken care of before it gets infected." She turned on the hot water, then pulled his forearm forward bringing his chest against her back. The contact momentarily rattled her. His nearness weakened her knees and wrapped her in his unique scent—sawdust and spice. It was like being held in his arms again, safe and sheltered.

She swallowed and heard Shaw inhale slowly.

"It's really not a big deal, Lainie. I'm fine."

He was so close his breath tickled her neck. "Stop being such a man."

"I am a man."

Oh, she was very aware of that. Too aware. Mentally, she bulldozed her thoughts back into line. Placing her hand under the faucet, she tested the water's temperature, then pulled a clean cloth from the drawer and dampened it. When she touched it to his arm, he sucked in a sharp breath. She looked over her shoulder at him. "I'm sorry." The dark blue eyes softened and he leaned his head closer.

"I'll live. Thanks to you."

Lainie forced her attention back to the injury, trying not to get distracted by his firm, tanned skin and corded muscles. The scratch was deep. She dabbed at the skin, trying to be gentle, but the blood had tangled in the dark hairs on his arm. She tugged his arm under the faucet to loosen the blood. The motion pressed them both against the counter. It would be so easy to turn and slip into his warm embrace.

No. She needed to concentrate on his wound. The scratch was clean, but still red and ugly. How could he not have known he'd hurt himself? "You should be more careful."

She dried his arm, taking more time than necessary before releasing him. He stepped back, creating space between them. She opened a drawer and removed a tube of antibacterial ointment. She handed it to him. It was not a good idea to keep holding his arm. Not with her emotions swirling like a category two hurricane.

Shaw held her gaze a moment before holding up the tube. "You always have first-aid equipment around the kitchen?"

"I have two little girls. One of them always has a cut or a scrape of some kind."

Shaw applied the cream then took her hand in his and laid the tube in her palm. He didn't let go. "Thank you for caring about me."

The intensity of his dark gaze rattled her already-shaky emotions. She glanced away, focusing instead on opening a large bandage and placing it over the cut. "Shaw, please be careful. I don't want you to get hurt."

"I'll be extra careful." He touched a finger to her forehead, trailing it down her temple and cupping the side of her face in his palm. "I don't want to see a frown on your lovely face." He tilted her face upward and kissed her cheek lightly.

Lainie fought to keep her senses about her. Now was the time. She had to say it before she lost her nerve. The longer she waited, the harder it would be. "Do you have a minute? I'd like to talk to you about something."

"Of course. What's on your mind?"

He'd leaned against the counter, thumbs latched into his belt. "It's about our discussion the other day, about the accident." She dared a look and saw his eyes had turn troubled. She plunged ahead before he could speak. "I've done a lot of soul-searching since then. Remembering things that I guess I buried or chose to forget. My husband didn't like following orders or rules, and sometimes that got him into trouble. I know you did all you could to keep him safe. I don't blame you for what happened."

"Why are you telling me this now?"

"Because it's time for me to let go of the past. I've spent too much time there. I want to look forward to getting the library done and starting a new life and a new future."

"Is that the only reason?"

What would he say if she told him she was starting to care for him? "And because we're friends now, and I don't want you to carry a burden you don't deserve." She waited for him to say something. But he remained silent, staring at her with an odd expression she couldn't interpret. The warmth in his eyes faded and became distant. He stepped away, rolling down his shirtsleeve before looking at her again.

"Thank you. And for what it's worth, I've finally been able to forgive myself, too."

He walked out without another word, leaving her puzzled and feeling slightly foolish. She'd expected him to be pleased, even relieved. She'd thought it would bring them closer, but she'd seen the walls go up behind his eyes. He was shutting her out. If he had forgiven himself, did that mean he no longer felt responsible for her? Was he letting her know he was moving on or reminding her he was a bachelor and not to get any ideas?

Had he somehow guessed her feelings? Or had he simply seen her affection in her eyes. How stupid could she get?

Shaw placed the hinge in the face frame of the cabinet, making sure it matched up with the positioning marks he'd made, then screwed it in with his cordless drill. He'd managed to coordinate the painters and floor refinishers so that one crew would work on the second floor of the library while the other worked on the main floor. Once their work was done, they would switch out and complete the job. It had saved him nearly three days. Breathing space before the deadline.

Today, he'd chosen to work in his shop helping Jeb finish the cabinetry. It had been a while since he'd worked on furniture. A good diversion from putting down baseboards and keeping half a dozen subcontractors in line. A good diversion from Lainie, too.

Thoughts of her had kept him up late. Not that unusual, but last night, he'd had to come to grips with the fact she'd forgiven him. He was relieved, but on the heels of that came the realization there was nothing holding him back from loving her. The accident was no longer a dark cloud looming between them.

Things had changed. Or at least, they had the potential to change. She'd come to like him, and maybe even respect him, to a point. He suspected she was attracted to him. The air crackled when they were close, and sometimes he saw emotions in her eyes that led him to believe she cared. But maybe that was wishful thinking on his part. There'd been no indication she wanted anything more than a friendship. Until last night.

Something had changed. He'd sensed a shift in her attitude.

So what happened now? He attached the top and bottom hinges to the cabinet door, then slid them into the brackets and locked them down.

His primary role was protector. They might have set the past aside, but until the library was finished, and Lainie officially installed as librarian, he was responsible for her and the girls. Any kind of romantic notions, real or imagined, were off-limits. It was a matter of honor.

But it was also a matter of the heart. His heart wanted one thing, his head another. If something developed with Lainie, was he ready? Or even capable? Would she walk away like the others? Would she expect something from him he couldn't provide? The way Vicki had. Things he still didn't understand.

He moved to the next cabinet, picked up a set of hinges and screwed them in place. He was getting ahead of himself. They were friends. He might care for her, but there was little chance she'd come to care for him in the same way. Even if she no longer blamed him for the accident, she would still look at him and see the past. He would always be a reminder of what she'd lost. Nothing would change that fact. Ever.

Anxiety continued to swirl in his stomach. He hadn't realized until now that Lainie's animosity toward him had acted like a safety barrier. As long as she resented him, blamed him, he didn't have to worry where his feelings would lead. Now he was exposed.

He glanced at his arm and the fresh bandage he'd applied this morning. Her tender care last night had nearly been his undoing. He liked that she worried about him, that she wanted him to be safe. He'd yearned to take her in his arms and kiss her senseless. But then he'd seen the door to a future open, and it had scared him back to reality.

Shaw fastened the last cabinet door in place and reached for the next, nearly bumping into Russ. "What are you doing here?"

"I was going to ask you the same thing. You hiding out?"

"Helping out. Big difference." When his friend didn't respond, Shaw dared a glance over his shoulder. He knew the look on the man's face. He wouldn't budge until Shaw talked. He put down his drill and leaned against the workbench. "Lainie told me she's forgiven me. She doesn't hold me responsible anymore."

Russ nodded in approval. "That's good. Maybe now you can stop trying to work off your guilt and let the woman know how you feel."

Shaw straightened and turned away, picking up the drill again. "Not happening. Until the library is done, I'm responsible for her well-being."

Russ scowled.

"I failed once. I'm not sure I want to make another mistake. Besides, I'm not ready to give up my freedom."

Russ rolled his eyes. "You mean like drinking with your buddies on the weekends, a string of beautiful women on your arm, no one to care what you do or where you go?"

"Come on. You know that's not me."

"So what exactly would you be giving up?"

He had no answer.

Russ patted him on the shoulder, the gesture fatherly. "It's time you stopped thinking of life as something to be conquered and start thinking of it as an adventure. And what good is the trip without someone to hold your hand along the way?"

Shaw picked up another set of hinges, fisting them in his palm. Everyone thought they had the answer, the simple solution to one's problems. But his relationship with Lainie wasn't simple. There would be no quick fix for him where she and her girls were concerned.

Lord, I know You know what You're doing here, but I sure wish You'd let me in on it.

He wanted a happy ending, but he'd learned those were few and far between in real life.

The dust motes in the attic of Shaw's old house floated on the late-morning sunlight, streaming through the small gable window. With her Saturday free from the library, Lainie had grabbed the opportunity to explore the attic for treasures to decorate the house, and maybe a chair for the front porch so she could enjoy her morning coffee.

Thanks to Millie's help, they had nearly finished inputting the collection, and the first shipment of lending books had started to arrive. Worried that Lainie was working too hard, Millie had announced she would handle things and ordered Lainie to take the weekend to rest, enjoy her children and do something fun. She'd delivered her decree in a tone that dared Lainie to refuse.

She had to admit, she needed a break, and she'd made the most of the day so far. She'd slept until the girls had awakened, snuggled with them in her bed, made flower-shaped pancakes for the girls and a bone-shaped one for Beaux. After promising lunch at Angelo's pizza, she'd convinced the girls to play in their room while she went up to the attic to explore.

She wondered how Shaw's arm was doing today. If he was like most men, he'd forget to put on a fresh bandage. She'd have to check on him later. She'd intended to do that this morning, but he'd already left by the time she had got up. The girls were missing him.

They hadn't seen him in a few days, and they talked about him constantly.

Shaw had backed away from them. Fine with her. Her dependence on him had got out of hand. He was so quick to step in and fix things and handle problems, she'd foolishly read more into his help than was intended.

She had little experience in the romance department. She was as susceptible to the old McKinney charm as every other woman. He'd planted a road sign clearly labeled Bachelorville. Take alternate route. Too late. He'd taken over her thoughts, and her heart was teetering near the edge.

At work, she glanced out the carriage house windows, hoping to catch a glimpse of him during the day. When she did, she stared in rapt infatuation. She liked to watch him work, the way he moved, the stern look on his face as he spoke with his men, and the way he would always run his fingers through his thick wavy hair after he'd removed his hard hat. And the sound of his voice never failed to shoot through her like fireworks.

She needed to be sensible. Even if there was a remote chance for a relationship, how could she reconcile that with her daughters? What would she tell them? She'd set herself up for heartbreak all over again, but now it included her children, too. The girls adored him.

Picking her way carefully around the wooden floors, she kept her eyes peeled for a chair she could take downstairs. So far, she'd found old bed frames, several wooden tables, rugs, trunks and pictures, but no chairs. Turning her attention to the other side of the attic, she uttered a soft squeal of delight. There, in the corner, tucked underneath boxes were two wicker rockers. One was in pristine condition, its weave tight and firm, the rockers smooth and secure. All it needed was a good cleaning and a fresh coat of paint. The other was usable, but in need of minor repairs on the arm and a new rocker to replace the broken one. Shaw could fix it, no problem.

She grasped the arms of the good chair, dropping it back down. It was heavier than it looked. There was no way she could maneuver it down the narrow attic stairs. She'd have to ask Shaw to bring them down when he got home. Her gaze fell on a small table nearby. It looked like a match to the chairs. That she could manage on her own. The table was lightweight, with a round top and legs that angled out from the center. It was lovely, and the perfect size to hold her Bible and a cup of coffee.

Lainie started down the stairs, peering around the tabletop so she could see the steps, which made a sharp turn at the bottom. As she neared the landing, her foot slipped out from under her. She dropped the table, grabbed for the wall, but tumbled forward instead. She stretched out her arm to stop her forward motion. Her arm hit the wall. White-hot pain shot up her arm to her elbow.

She screamed.

When she opened her eyes, she lay in a heap at the bottom of the stairs, her feet in the hallway, her shoulder wedged against the last step and the little table. Pain like a hundred knives pierced her arm. Tears spilled down her cheeks.

"Mommy!"

Natalie's voice pulled her from her confusion. She looked into her child's worried face. Chrissy hunkered down, starting to cry. "Mommy?"

Forcing herself to ignore the pain, she tried to think logically. "I'm all right, but I need you to go get Miss Gwen. Can you do that?"

Natalie nodded, her blue eyes fearful.

"Tell her I fell."

Natalie ran off. Chrissy sat beside her and patted her shoulder. "It'll be okay, Mommy. I promise. Be brave."

If she didn't hurt so badly, she would have laughed. Her child had said the words with the same intonation as she herself did when trying to comfort her daughters.

Lainie attempted to shift her position, but any movement sent searing pain along her elbow and forearm. *Please Lord, let Gwen be home. I need help.*

Natalie had barely left when pounding footsteps shook the floor. "Lainie!"

Shaw. Relief washed through her, removing much of her fear. She didn't know why he was here in the middle of the day, but his presence gave her great comfort. Shaw could fix anything. He knelt beside her, his eyes filled with fear and concern.

"*Mon cher*, what happened?" His eyes raked over her with concern.

"I was trying to bring this table down and I slipped. I think I broke my arm."

"Can you sit up if I help you?"

"I don't know. What are you doing here?"

"I left one of my tools in the garage." Shaw took her left arm and gently eased her around until she was sitting on the bottom step. She tried to move her arm only to cry out in pain.

"We need to get you to the clinic."

She looked at her daughters. Natalie was staring wide-eyed with fear. Chrissy pouted and sniffled.

Shaw touched Natalie's shoulder. "Girls, I need to take your mom to a doctor so he can fix her arm. I want you to go next door and tell Miss Gwen what happened. Tell her I'm taking your mom to the clinic, and I'll call her later. Can you do that?"

Natalie nodded. "Yes, sir."

"Good. Take your sister's hand and go straight to Miss Gwen's."

With the girls on their way, Shaw turned his attention back to her. "I'm going to stabilize your arm. Do you have a scarf?"

She nodded. "In my room, the top drawer."

He returned and folded the scarf into a simple sling. He took hold of her wrist and carefully raised it against her chest. She tried not to cry out, but failed.

With her arm secured, Shaw scooped her up in his arms and carried her to his truck, placing her gently in the front seat. She barely remembered the ride to the clinic. The only thing that was clear in her mind was Shaw's holding her hand, and his repeated words of comfort. He had a nice deep voice. Like a rich alto sax. Mentally, she giggled. That was silly. One thing pricked at her thoughts. "Why do you keep saying Shaw over and over?" She thought she heard him chuckle softly.

"I'm not. I'm saying *cher*. It's Cajun for dear, or darling."

She smiled. "It sounds like Sha."

"Yes, it does."

"That's nice." Her mind was fuzzy through the first part of the examination. She tried to concentrate on what the doctor was telling her. Hyperextended elbow. Not broken. Immobilize. Pain meds. No lifting. Week to ten days.

Full realization of her predicament didn't hit until she was back in Shaw's truck and heading home. "Did he say I had to wear this for two weeks?" She stared at the blue brace cradling her injured elbow. She was thinking clearly now, but unfortunately that brought a mental list of the things she wouldn't be able to do.

"He said a week to ten days if you rest and take care of your arm. That means no lifting."

Lainie swallowed a lump of disappointment. That meant she couldn't hold her daughters for over a week. Natalie was almost too big for her to lift, but Chrissy was still small and liked to sit on her lap and cuddle in the morning. A new and more disturbing thought sent her heart racing. "The books. Does that mean I can't work on the books?"

"Not until the sling comes off. Even then, you might have to go easy."

Anxiety squeezed her chest. "I have to work at the library. You know what will happen if we're not ready by the deadline." Heartsick, she rested her head against the back of the seat. "I can't believe this is happening now, just when we're getting on top of things."

"Millie will help."

"It takes both of us working together. She can't do that work alone."

"She'll have to. You can oversee the work until your arm heals."

"Sit back and supervise others? Not me."

"You don't have a choice."

Tears stung the backs of her eyes. "Why now?"

Shaw squeezed her hand. "It'll be all right. I can help with the girls and Gwen will be next door when I'm not home."

As they pulled into the driveway, Gwen hurried across the front lawn.

"How bad is it?"

Lainie explained, receiving a gentle touch on her good shoulder from her friend. "You don't worry about a thing. I'm right next door. Just call. The girls can stay with me for the next few days so you can rest."

"Thank you, Gwen, but I need them with me. I'll be fine, and I promise to call if I need you. Can you send them home? I know they're worried about me."

Gwen nodded in agreement. "They've asked about you every five minutes. Oh, and Millie called. She said not to worry. She's activating the former Friends of the Library volunteers to come and help."

Shaw lightly touched her back, urging her toward the door. "You need to lie down. The pain shot the nurse gave you will make you drowsy."

Lainie allowed Shaw to help her upstairs and get her settled on the bed, making sure she had what she needed. He'd just placed a glass of water on the nightstand when the girls ran in, their blue eyes sparkling.

"Mommy! You're home. We missed you."

Chrissy stared at the sling. "Is your arm hurt?"

"Yes, but it'll be better soon. I have to wear this so my arm won't move. I can't lift you up or drive my car or do a lot of the things I usually do. I'll need you and your sister to be my helpers for the next week or so. Can you do that?"

Two little heads nodded rapidly. "I can make the bed." Natalie smiled.

"I can fix supper."

Chrissy's confidence made Lainie smile. "You can? That's a big help. What will you fix?"

"Pop-Tarts."

"My favorite."

Shaw smiled and bent down to the girls. "Mommy needs to sleep for a while. Let's go downstairs and make a list of things we can do to help while her arm gets better."

"I love you, Mommy."

"Me, too."

Lainie lay back against the pillows, the number of obstacles in her path growing larger every second. How would she give the girls their baths? She couldn't wash their hair with only one arm. And what about Shaw's bookkeeping? Could she manage his accounts with only five fingers to tap the keys? Most importantly, how would she keep things moving at the library?

She closed her eyes, feeling the tug of sleep as the pain medication took hold. There was only one answer. She'd have to learn to do everything one-handed. She'd become a lefty. A southpaw. Easy-peasy. Her eyes grew heavy and she sank into the fluffy cloud of her mind. And how was she going to kiss Shaw with one hand in a sling? Where had that thought come from?

Her eyes closed, releasing visions of Shaw scooping her up and carrying her down the stairs as if she weighed nothing. She knew better, but he'd held her close. Even in her pain she had felt secure and safe. Cherished. *Cher.* She liked the sound of it. She liked the way he said it. *Sha.*

Funny how pain meds distorted things.

Chapter Nine

Shaw had never known a Sunday morning like this. Instead of a cup of coffee and the Sunday *Dispatch* before church, he was sitting in Lainie's kitchen running a beauty parlor.

He twisted a red stretchy band around the clump of yellow hair he'd pulled to the side of Chrissy's head, feeling all thumbs and dumb as dirt. The little girl waited patiently while he tugged the other side of her hair upward and secured it with a blue band. He frowned. Something wasn't right. Chrissy whirled and smiled at him.

"Thank you, Misser Shaw. You don't hurt my head the way Mommy does."

He supposed that was a good thing except— "Your ponytails aren't even." One was at least two inches higher and farther to the back.

"That's okay. I'm just going to play outside." She skipped off.

Natalie stopped at his side, holding out her hand for the brush. "I can do my own hair. I'm six, you know."

Shaw stifled a grin. "I heard that." He handed her the

brush, wondering what Lainie would say if she could see her daughters. They'd spent the night at Gwen's so Lainie could get the rest she needed after her fall, but she hadn't been happy about the arrangement. She'd wanted the girls with her. He'd finally convinced her they'd be safer next door. If something happened, she might be too drugged to respond. He insisted on leaving Beaux with her just as a precaution, though Shaw himself had barely slept, listening for any unusual sound from her side of the house.

Gwen had brought the girls to his place early this morning. They were eager to see their mother, so after a promise to be quiet and not wake her, he'd settled them into the kitchen.

Breakfast had been a new adventure. After deflecting demands from Natalie and her little sister for cookies, chocolate, candy and pizza, he'd finally convinced them cereal and juice was a much better idea. He was feeling pretty triumphant about his accomplishment. He'd even managed to get them to clean up afterward, but only after promising to push them "up to the sky" in the swings.

"Good morning."

Shaw glanced up to see Lainie coming down the stairs, Beaux leading the way. She looked pale, but her eyes were clear, and her dark hair was pleasingly mussed from sleep. "How are you feeling?"

"Sore, achy and totally foolish." She gave him a little smile. "I should have watched where I was going."

Shaw pulled out a chair for her. "Coffee?" She nodded. "It's an old house and those steps weren't built to today's codes. They're too narrow and steep."

Lainie took the coffee cup, added a dash of milk and a packet of sweetener. "Where are the girls?"

"Swings." He sat beside her. "I promised to push them. Gwen offered to take them to church, but I thought you'd rather have them here when you woke up."

She ran a hand through her thick hair, mussing it further and making him want to bury his fingers in the beautiful strands. He settled for laying his hand on hers. "I'm glad you're going to be okay. You scared me senseless, you know."

"I scared myself." She clutched her mug between her hands, her brown eyes troubled. "How am I going to work, or take care of the girls with my right arm out of commission? Just getting out of bed this morning was a challenge."

"I've got it all worked out. Gwen will be on call to take the girls or come and help you with personal things. I'll be here in the evenings and mornings to help, and I plan on coming by during the day to check on you."

Lainie shook her head. "You can't take that much time off from work. The deadline is getting closer."

"We're in good shape. I can afford the time to make sure you're okay." He looked into her brown eyes, feeling the pull of her sweetness. Maybe, once he was free from his promise, he'd tell her how he felt and see where things went from there. Right now, neither one of them was willing to acknowledge the feelings stirring beneath the surface.

She smiled. "Thank you. You're a good friend, Shaw."

Disappointment tightened his chest. That was him. A good friend. He didn't like the title much, but it was safer that way. He stood. "I'd better go push those girls before I get tossed out of the Princess Club. Call if you need anything."

Shaw returned to his own kitchen, taking a moment to fill Beaux's water dish. He needed distance from Lainie. He'd always backed away when things became too serious. He liked being single. Not having to answer to anyone suited him. Lainie was right. He left women before they could leave him—like his mom and Vicki. Lainie was the kind of woman he had always dreamed of, but the reality was he'd tried a long-term relationship and failed. But now he was faced with someone who would never walk away. That scared him more than anything.

What if Vicki was right and his heart was so tightly locked away, he'd never be able to give it to someone else? Not even Lainie. Then she would walk away, too. He'd had too many women walk out of his life. He didn't need three more.

Lainie carried her drink to the door, only to realize she'd have to put it down to open it. Life with one arm incapacitated was way more complicated than she'd expected. Shaw had gone to the library to check on the job, and she'd promised to be careful while he was gone. After maneuvering things around, she took a seat on the back porch to watch the girls play. Midday on a glorious Sunday. There was a long list of things she'd like to do, but she couldn't do a one. She'd missed church. Then she'd tried to push the girls in the swings, but with one arm, she'd only made them swing crooked. And to top things off, she wasn't even dressed yet. She'd need help for that. Maybe she'd stay in her pj's all day. Just because. The sight of Gwen walking across the lawn with a covered dish in her hands brightened her mood considerably.

Gwen smiled and raised the dish. "Chicken and noodles. The girls eat it at my house so I'm sure it won't go to waste."

"Thank you. That's very thoughtful."

"Pastor Jim announced you on the prayer chain in church this morning. You'll be getting meals from everyone in the congregation."

Lainie tilted her head. "Don't be too sure. I'm still not the most popular newcomer, remember?"

"That is not true. Everyone is delighted with your efforts to get the library done on time."

After putting the casserole inside, Gwen joined Lainie on the porch glider. "You feeling better today? I was so glad to hear you hadn't broken your arm when you fell."

"Me, too. I thought for sure I had."

"Don't worry about anything. Shaw and I have you covered. He's a real sweetheart. You know that, don't you?"

"I do. He's a good friend."

"Speaking of friends, I want to thank you for giving me the courage to face my mother."

"What do you mean?"

Gwen fidgeted with her hands. "My mother can be very opinionated. She truly believes she knows what's best for everyone else. It's been easier for me to just go along and not make waves. But then I met you, and I saw how brave you were, how you fought for your job at the library no matter how big the obstacle."

"Oh, Gwen, That wasn't bravery. That was desperation. For my girls. You would do the same thing for your boys."

She smiled. "But that's just it. I didn't. It was because of you that I had the courage to confront my mom and Millie about their attitudes."

"I never meant to cause trouble for you."

Gwen smiled and grasped her hand. "You didn't. Things between my mom and me have changed. We're talking more. And being honest with one another. I even told her I want to go back to work in the fall when the boys are in school. She believes a mother should be in the home with the children."

"If you're serious, I have the budget to hire two more employees for the library." She would love having Gwen working with her. "Millie will be working part-time, but that leaves a full-time and another part-time slot available."

"Keep that application for me. I think I'll take you up on that."

After helping Lainie shower and get dressed, Gwen said goodbye, but not before offering to take the girls later so Lainie could rest. She thanked the Lord for such kind and generous friends. Her welcome to Dover hadn't been a good one, but day by day, He had placed people in her life to help when she needed it. Like Gwen and Millie. But mostly Shaw.

He was dependable, always there, smoothing things out, solving problems, comforting her. But it was his motivation she questioned. Was he still feeling obligated? Was there a small part of him helping because he cared? She hoped so. She wanted him to care because her heart was losing the battle. She was falling in love with him, and she didn't know how to stop it.

And she needed to. Her emotions felt new and frightening. For so long, she'd been locked up in a vault of the past, denying her feelings, pouring herself into work and caring for her daughters.

Now she wanted to break free and participate in life again and embrace emotions she'd thought dead forever. But letting go felt like she was throwing away an important part of her life. How long should she hold on to the past? When was it okay to let go and move on? Could she move on and still cherish her memories?

She didn't have an answer. Yet. The Lord had promised to be a light unto her path, not a floodlight illuminating all her answers. For now, she'd take it one day at a time, focus on her job. The rest would sort itself out.

Shaw balanced the bag of delicious-smelling burgers and the tray of drinks and tapped his foot against Lainie's back door. As he'd expected, Natalie and Chrissy wasted no time in opening the door for him. They were always waiting when he got home each night, eager to see him and curious about what he'd brought for supper. Lainie found it difficult to cook with only one arm, and he had little time to spare, so for the past few nights, he'd stopped on the way home and bought supper. It wasn't the healthiest diet, but a few fast-food meals wouldn't hurt.

After placing the bags on the table, he opened his arms for his welcome home. This had become his favorite part of the day. Chrissy liked to be picked up so she could kiss his cheek. Natalie hugged his waist and gave him her best dimpled smile. He'd nicknamed her Sparkle because she was always happy. Beaux, always the gentleman, waited for his turn for a scratch behind the ears.

Since Lainie's accident, he'd been drawn deeper into their lives. It had been both terrifying and fascinating. He'd found it easiest to simply go along rather than try and do things logically. Apparently, little princesses and their mommy had their own unique way of dealing with life.

Strangely enough, he found he liked the female energy, and he learned more about Lainie than he'd thought possible. He'd learned that she liked her coffee sweet, but her tea with only lemon. She liked to keep her home neat and orderly, but didn't mind if the Princess Club was a giant mess. He'd also managed to get Chrissy's ponytails even.

Lainie entered the kitchen and took a seat at the table. "That smells wonderful. I'm starved."

Her smile momentarily derailed his thoughts. She looked adorable in shorts and a bright red T-shirt. He wanted to ask for a welcome-home hug from her, too. It took all his effort to right his wayward thoughts. "Dig in while it's hot."

She looked so much better than when he'd found her crumpled at the bottom of the stairs. She had been pale and shaking, her eyes dull and filled with pain. They'd regained much of their sparkle, but he could see the tiny lines of worry and discomfort around the edges of her mouth. She was still hurting some. Thankfully, she was following doctor's orders, but Shaw also knew she was anxious to get back to work. Millie told him she checked in three or four times a day.

He ate in silence, letting the sense of family wrap around him. The girls chattered about things they'd done and told stories about Beaux. Lainie listened as if every word from her daughters' mouths was of vital importance. She occasionally gave him a wink or a nod to share a point of amusement.

How nice it would be to come home to his own family, to take care of them, to provide for them. This was something he understood. This was his strength. Taking charge, being responsible and fixing problems.

He had learned how to manage his dad's moods, when to leave him alone and when to push him back into life. During the good times, Shaw would step back and watch as his dad found the next woman he believed would make him happy. But Shaw knew eventually she would leave, as well, and the cycle would start over again.

"I don't need you to take care of me. I need you to love me."

He hadn't understood what Vicki had meant. He still didn't. He had loved her. They'd had so much in common. Getting married had seemed the logical thing to do. So why hadn't it worked?

He glanced around the table at Lainie and the girls. Until he knew the answer to that question, he couldn't think about a future with anyone. Because if Vicki was right and his heart was locked up, then Lainie would leave, too, and that would be more painful than all the guilt he'd carried about the accident.

Shaw pulled his focus to the burger in his hand. His appetite was gone. He realized with a start that everyone had finished eating but him.

"Will you push us now, Misser Shaw?"

Eager to escape his thoughts, he tossed the rest of his

meal into the bag. "Sure. Let's go. I've got a few minutes before I have to go back to the library."

Lainie raised an eyebrow. "Still more to do tonight?"

He thought he saw disappointment in her eyes. Had she wanted him to stay home tonight? "Always. I'll be back in time to help put the girls to bed."

She laid a hand on his arm, sending warmth along his skin. He looked into her eyes and was filled with longing to kiss her and never stop.

"Are you all right?" she asked. "You seem troubled."

He liked that she cared about him, that she noticed his moods. He rested his hand on the side of her face, his thumb gently stroking the soft cheek. "No. Just trying to stay on top of things. That deadline is getting closer."

"I know, and you've lost time from the job by taking care of things here. I really appreciate it, though."

She was so close, so lovely, he knew he should step back and leave but his feet were nailed to the floor. He lowered his head, his gaze riveted to her slightly parted lips. He'd wondered too long. He had to know.

She didn't resist as he tilted her face upward and took possession of her lips. He wanted to consume her, but he allowed himself only one small taste. He wasn't disappointed. The sweetness of the kiss, the warmth of her, fulfilled all his dreams.

He pulled away, his gaze locked with hers. He saw the same emotion in her brown eyes that swirled through him. There was no denying the attraction was mutual.

A lance of fear sliced along his nerves. Fear of failure, fear of being unable to love her the way she deserved. He saw fear in her eyes, too, the one he dreaded. No matter what she might feel for him, she would always see him first and foremost through the lens of the past.

She stepped back. "Shaw maybe this isn't—"

"It's just a kiss between friends. That's all. I'd, uh, better go. There's too much riding on this job for both of us."

He walked out, kicking himself three ways from Sunday for crossing a barrier he'd sworn to defend. It was a good thing Lainie was going back to work tomorrow. He needed to rebuild some walls before it was too late.

Lainie stared out the window in Shaw's truck as he drove her to the library. She couldn't stay home another day. Her arm was feeling better, and she was impatient to get back to work. Even if that meant sitting on the sidelines and supervising.

She stole a glance at Shaw. He'd been quiet and distant all morning. She'd anticipated his kiss for a long time now, and it had met all her expectations. Though brief and gentle, she sensed the undercurrent, the emotion he was keeping firmly in check.

But when the kiss had ended, he'd shut down, his cobalt eyes had turned navy, and she'd sensed his withdrawal. Her heart still smarted from his blunt reminder that it was only a kiss between friends. It had meant nothing to him.

She shouldn't read too much into it. The most eligible bachelor in Dover was skilled at pouring on the charm, teasing the ladies with that knee-buckling smile and making a woman feel as if she were the only one in the universe.

She swallowed. The attraction between them was

growing. The kiss had proved that. She just didn't know what to do about it. Falling for Shaw was guaranteed heartbreak.

Shaw pulled the truck to a stop near the carriage house. He looked over at her, his eyes filled with questions. "Are you sure you're ready for this?"

"I'm fine. I need to be here. We're too close to the deadline."

"Okay." He squeezed her hand. "But I've already told Millie and her crew to make sure you don't do more than you're able. And they *will* come and get me if you do, and I'll take you right back home."

Lainie slipped her hand from his and reached across her lap to open the door. "In case you haven't noticed, I've become very adept at being a lefty. There's a lot I can do with only one hand that will still be helpful." She smiled at him before shutting the truck door. "I'll be fine. Don't worry about me."

She stepped into the carriage house and was met with a warm hug from Millie.

"I should send you home, but it's so good to have you back, I just can't. However, you'd better not overdo it."

"I got the same speech from Shaw." She smiled at the other women who had gathered around. Millie began the introductions. "Lainie, meet your Friends of the Library volunteers."

Ellen Bower, an older woman with a friendly face, was the first to step forward. "I've heard so much about you. I'm Shelby Durrant's grandmother. I think you've met her?"

"Yes, I have."

A slender woman with salt-and-pepper hair introduced herself as Carol Stanton. "I'm not officially a

Friend, but I wanted to come and help. The people of Dover were so generous to me and my husband last winter when a storm destroyed our home. They rebuilt the entire house in a matter of weeks."

Millie reached out her hand to indicate a woman in her late seventies, who walked with a cane. "This is Edith Johnson. She bakes the best chocolate chip cookies in the county."

"I'm an avid reader. Always have been. Give me a good mystery and I'm a happy camper. You'll get sick of seeing me here when it opens."

Lainie laughed. "Never."

"And this is Myra Latimer. She and her husband own the local office supply store here in Dover."

Lainie was touched deeply by the generosity of these women. "Thank you, ladies, for helping out. We couldn't get the library open if it weren't for you."

Edith smiled. "We're happy to help, but as you can see, the lending books are starting to arrive, and we're running out of space. Some of the furniture is here, too. We need to find a place to keep it until we're open."

Millie waved her hand in dismissal. "Not to worry. I've already solved our problem. Dutch Ingles has an empty old building one block over. He keeps saying he'll find a great new business to lease it to, but he never will. I talked him into letting us store the sorted volumes there, and he offered to come and pick them up for us when they're ready. He also owns a nice big van."

Carol looked puzzled. "That's remarkable. How did you manage that?"

Ellen snickered. "Remarkable my big toe. Dutch has had a thing for Millie for years, but she won't give him so much as a wink."

Lainie arched her eyebrows. "Millie, I'm seeing a whole new side to you."

Millie raised her chin. "Can I help it if I have magnetism?"

The comment elicited chuckles and a groan from her friends.

The women got back to work, but it didn't take Lainie long to realize there was little she could do with only one hand. Typing was too slow when she had to hunt and peck each key, and unboxing books wasn't as easy as she'd thought it would be. Pushing back from the computer, she uttered a groan of frustration.

Millie came to her side. "Not as easy as you thought?"

Lainie's shoulders sagged. "I'm useless."

"That is not true." Carol Stanton wagged a finger. "Millie tells us you have all kinds of wonderful ideas for things to do once we open."

"I do, and I've had plenty of time to think up more these last few days."

"Well, don't keep them a secret." Myra joined them at the small table they used as a desk.

As Lainie shared her plans and ideas with the volunteers, her excitement and confidence grew. She couldn't wait to be settled in the new building. She looked forward to helping people find books, teaching them to use the computer and offering lectures and book signings.

Ellen chuckled softly. "You sound like Millie used to. Always coming up with things to draw people to the library."

Lainie's heart warmed with the compliment. "I think Millie and I both want the same thing for Dover—an active, vital library to serve the community."

Myra shook her head. "I hate to spoil the moment, but some folks are losing interest in the library. They're saying it's taking too long and that it might not even open."

Lainie was horrified. "Of course it will happen. Shaw is working practically around the clock to make the deadline."

"I know, but it wouldn't hurt to do a little promotion. My daughter Nicki literally saved our store with her marketing ideas. I was thinking we could take some of these children's books to the senior center on the square and have them read to the children during the day. With school out for the summer, I know moms would welcome something like that to fill the time."

"Myra, you're brilliant." Millie faced Lainie. "Promotion is something you can do even with your arm in a sling."

Lainie liked the idea. "Yes. I'll make posters to put around town announcing some of the programs we'll have. And I can leave these library card applications in the stores for people to fill out. We could put a drop-in box at the courthouse, and then we can have people's library cards ready and waiting on opening day."

With her hope renewed and her sense of purpose restored, Lainie picked up several children's books and a packet of applications, and slipped them into a small canvas bag. "Since I can't do much here, I'm going to become a walking advertisement." She would make this library a success and a place to come and enjoy books and learn, to spend time with friends and to fall in love with reading.

If enthusiasm alone was a guarantee, the Dover Library would be a success. But right now, it depended on Shaw getting his part done. Truthfully, the library could open without books, but not without the inspector's final approval. All Lainie could do was press on.

Shaw laid the last shelf onto the support cleat in the storage closet, mentally checking off another task on his list. One by one, the details were being addressed. The floors had been refinished and covered with paper to protect them. Carpet was going down in the reading corner and children's area in the morning. The final elevator inspection was done and approved. Things were moving forward, but not fast enough to suit him.

The new bookshelves would be delivered and installed starting Monday, but that still left a long list of small jobs to complete, not to mention bringing in the furniture Lainie had ordered. And of course all the books. He'd been shocked when she'd told him the building would house more than thirty thousand books. His mind couldn't begin to fathom that amount. But he could easily understand Lainie's excitement at the thought of all those volumes under her protection.

Since Lainie had returned to work, Shaw had pulled back on helping out at home. She'd adapted to the sling and managed to find ways of doing several tasks one-handed.

He still planned his time around being home for supper, but he returned to work once he was sure everything was taken care of for the day. More time on the job was supposed to keep Lainie from invading his thoughts every moment. He'd even avoided going to the carriage house. But his heart wanted to be with her.

Shaw closed the closet door, scanning it one last time to make sure it was positioned perfectly in the frame, and the knob worked easily. Satisfied, he turned to see Russ striding in his direction. His solemn expression raised a twinge of concern.

"You got a minute?"

"Sure. What's up?"

Russ took a moment before he spoke, further raising Shaw's concern.

"It's Viola. She started having pain in her hands and arms last night. It got so bad she couldn't even hold a paper cup. I took her to the clinic. They think it might be the start of rheumatoid arthritis. I'm taking her to a specialist this afternoon for more tests."

"I'm so sorry to hear that. What do you need me to do?"

Russ removed his hard hat, ran a hand through his hair, then replaced it. "I know this is a lousy time to ask, but I need some time off. Maybe a week. I don't know how long it'll take to get the tests results back or what will have to happen after that."

Shaw squeezed the man's shoulder. "Don't give it a thought. Go. Take care of Viola first. I don't want you to think about this job until she's all right."

"But how will you make the deadline?"

Shaw steered the man toward the door. "Not your problem. I've got it under control."

Russ nodded, his eyes communicating that he knew Shaw was trying to make light of the situation.

Shaw watched the man disappear before exhaling a heavy sigh. He linked his hands behind his neck. The timing of this couldn't have been worse. Russ did the work of three men. Without him, Shaw was looking at even more hours on the job. The only thing left to give up was sleep. So be it.

By the end of the day, Shaw had reworked the construction schedule as best he could. Millie had taken Lainie home so he could stay on the job. When he pulled the truck into the drive, the headlights caught sight of someone on the front porch swing. Lainie. It was her favorite spot in the evening. In the morning, she favored the wicker chairs he'd painted and repaired for her. He'd retrieved them from the attic while she was at work and given them a quick fix-up and paint job and had surprised her when she'd got home. He'd received a hug for his efforts.

He joined her on the swing. Just sitting beside her calmed his worries. "I didn't expect you to still be up."

"I didn't expect you to be so late." She studied him a moment. "Something happened today, didn't it?"

"Is it that obvious? I lost my foreman today."

"Russ quit?"

"No. It's only a temporary leave. His wife is ill. She's having tests run and he wants to be with her. I agreed. That's more important. They think she may have RA. She's a seamstress, so something like this could change her life."

"I'll keep her in my prayers. What will this mean for the job?"

"I'll have to work longer hours."

She slipped her hand in his, the contact releasing the last of his tension. Amazing how just being with her made things better. "There aren't many hours in the day left."

"I know." He longed to pull her closer and lose himself in her warmth and compassion, but not yet. He would keep his word and his feelings in check. For now.

"What are you doing out here so late?" Her hesitation told him it was something she was reluctant to share.

"You know how I've been going around town promoting the library? Today I found a fistful of card applications tossed into a trash bin in front of the Magnolia Café. Why would someone do that?"

"I don't know. Most of the people I talk to are excited about the library reopening." He wrapped his arm around her shoulders. She rested her head in the crook of his shoulder. His heart beat erratically in his chest. Could she feel it? Did she know what she did to him? "Once the library is open, people will come around. Sometimes people get set in their ways and it's hard for them to let go." As he was?

Was he using his sense of responsibility as a barrier because his single life was too comfortable? Or was he afraid of failing and being hurt again?

"I hope you're right. I don't want to be an outsider forever."

Shaw held her tighter, resting his chin on her silky hair and inhaling the strawberry scent he'd come to love. "That will never happen. You're too warm and caring. People can see that from the moment they meet you. Plus, you have Millie on your side now."

"I hope you're right because I want to stay in Dover. I want to raise my girls here."

Shaw's heart swelled with hope. He wanted that, too. More than anything he'd ever wanted in his life.

Chapter Ten

Lainie ran her fingers over the stabilizing tape wrapped around her elbow. The doctor had been pleased with her progress and had allowed her to dispense with the sling and use the wrap instead. She'd promised him she'd not overuse her arm, and faithfully do the exercises he prescribed. To celebrate, Shaw had suggested they go to the Peace Community Church picnic and ice-cream social. The girls were so excited it was all she could do to keep them still during church.

She glanced at Shaw, sitting behind the wheel of her car. He must have sensed her watching him because he turned his head and smiled, sending her pulse racing. Sometimes when she looked at him, she forgot to breathe. His dark piercing eyes, dazzling smile and that dimple in the center of his chin made him hard to resist.

Having Shaw involved in their lives this past week had only deepened her feelings for him. His presence had also made her aware how incomplete she'd felt for the past few years. Sending him off to work each morning and sharing their evening meals had reminded her how much she missed the comforting predictability of married life. The sense of being a complete family.

But Shaw wasn't family, only a friend. He was the man who'd stepped in to help because he owed it to her. No other reason. They might have set the past aside and become friends, but for him, that was all it would ever be. She and the girls were an obligation, and once the library was open he'd be on his way without a backward glance.

Lainie faced the window, oblivious to the lovely day outside. If they made the deadline, she'd be unable to remain in the duplex. Shaw would want to start restoring his house so he could sell it. Heavy sadness shrouded her mind. She didn't like the thought of someone else living there. She'd come to think of the old house as her home.

But that was an issue for tomorrow. Today she was going to put all of those concerns aside and enjoy the picnic. She knew people in Dover now, and she was eager to start making deeper connections. Real friendships.

The parking lot at Friendship Park was full when they arrived, forcing Shaw to park along the street. "Are you sure we weren't supposed to bring something other than chairs?"

Shaw pulled the two lawn chairs from the trunk while she helped the girls out of the car, then picked up the small basket of picnic utensils.

"Nope. Everything is provided." They started across the easement to the main entrance of the park, and Lainie felt many of her concerns drift away. It was a beautiful day. Sunny, but not too humid, a few fluffy clouds dotted the blue sky, and a nice steady breeze kept things comfortable. Several people greeted them as they passed. A few stared and moved on. She tried not to think it was because of her.

"Lainie, I see a picnic table near the playground. Let's set up there, then we can watch the girls play."

She scanned the park as she spread the plastic cloth over the weathered wood. People played softball in the far field. Off to one side was a horseshoe pit and a cornhole toss. In the opposite field, a volleyball net had been erected. The food was set up on long tables under a row of large shade tents, and at the end, ten ice-cream freezers were busily churning the day's desserts. From the looks of things, every member of Peace Community was here. And then some.

Throughout the day, Lainie met the husbands and families of her library ladies, and Shaw introduced her to the rest of the Durrant clan. The loving family reinforced her desire for roots and permanence. Her parents had loved to move, see new places and explore new locations. She'd longed for the thread of connection that only staying in one place could provide.

The day passed too quickly, and before she knew it, the crowd was starting to thin. The hot dogs and hamburgers had all been eaten and the ice cream devoured. The people who still remained lounged by the small lake or on picnic tables waiting for a local band to start their performance. It had been a fun day and she wasn't ready for it to end. Neither were her daughters, who had made a few new friends and were making nonstop trips down the tall sliding board.

Shaw returned from disposing of their empty drink cups. "Are you up for a walk? The trails should be nice and cool this time of day."

A walk in the woods with Shaw was too tempting to resist. "I'm not sure the girls will want to leave the playground."

Shaw nodded at the table Gwen and Eric had claimed. "No problem. Gwen said she'd keep an eye on them."

The air was noticeably cooler the moment they stepped under the thick canopy of trees. A few yards ahead, the trail split into three directions. Shaw steered her down the path marked Camellia.

"Are you having fun?"

"Yes. Today, I actually feel like I belong."

"Is belonging important to you?"

"We moved a lot when I was growing up. I was always the new kid who never fit in. About the time I started to make friends, it was time to move again. I always dreamed of finding a place like this where I knew everyone and had a deep connection. I want that for my girls. I want them to grow up with the same friends and shared memories. I want them to have a place to return to even after they have families of their own."

She wanted something else, too. She wanted to spend each day with someone she loved, someone who loved her children as much as she did and who would love her forever. But that was something best kept to herself.

"I think you can find all that in Dover. I wasn't raised here, but I think of it as home."

"Where was home, originally?"

"Lafayette, Louisiana. After Mom left, Dad and I moved to Baton Rouge."

"Does he still live there?"

"He's in Florida with wife number five. Or is it six?" He shrugged. "Hard to keep track."

Shaw took her hand as they continued to stroll along

the shaded path. He was more relaxed than she'd ever seen him. She decided to ask the question that had puzzled her for a long time. "Why have you never married?" He didn't respond, but kept walking, holding her hand firmly in his. Maybe she shouldn't have asked.

"I came close once."

Lainie's heart tightened. "What happened?"

He took a deep breath. "She made it halfway down the aisle before turning and walking out of the church."

Lainie stopped and faced him, her heart aching with sadness. "Oh, Shaw, I'm so sorry. Did she tell you why?"

He nodded, but didn't look at her. "She said I wasn't engaged in the relationship. That I was more focused on my work than on her. She said she didn't want a marriage with a man who had his heart locked up."

Lainie squeezed his hand. How awful for a proud man like him to be left standing at the altar while his bride walked away. The way his mother had. "Was that true? I mean, did you love her?"

"Very much."

She could sense his old pain stirring beneath the surface. "She was wrong, you know. You do give your heart to everything you do. I've seen your dedication to your work, to your crew and to helping me and the girls. You're a good man. An honorable man."

Shaw's eyes darkened as he looked at her, and his hands took hold of her shoulders gently. "Have I mentioned you're good for my ego?"

Lainie chuckled softly. "I don't think your ego needs any help."

"Good for my heart, then." He pulled her close, sliding his arms around her waist and easing her against him.

Her insides melted along with her common sense.

She went willingly into his embrace, accepting his kiss with no hesitation. His lips were gentle, tender, almost reverent at first then his arms tightened, and she let herself be lost in the moment. She'd never been kissed like this before. Fierce yet gentle at the same time. A sweet sense of connection enfolded her heart, drawing them together in some mysterious way.

When he ended the kiss, her mind was a fuzzy blur of emotion and sensations. She searched his deep blue eyes, her hand moving up to touch the strong jaw.

He cradled her face between his work-roughened hands, caressing her with his dark blue gaze. He lowered his head and kissed her again, a brief, sure touch, as if claiming her for his own.

As her thoughts cleared, she saw the folly in what she'd done. Kissing Shaw would only complicate her already-conflicted emotions. But it had been a long time since she'd felt like a woman, a desirable, attractive woman. For now, that was enough.

Voices up the trail shattered the intimate moment, pulling them apart. A group of teenagers appeared around the curve ahead, laughing and joking. When they moved on, Shaw took her hand. "We'd better get back if we want to hear the band."

She'd been looking forward to the music, but it had lost its appeal. She needed to regroup and get her emotions under control. "I think I'd better take the girls home. They're worn-out and it'll be hard to get them to sleep tonight."

"All right."

She was glad Shaw kept her hand in his, but she couldn't help wondering what lay ahead for them down the path they were on.

* * *

Lainie rinsed the bowls and set them into the dishwasher that evening. She'd been right about having trouble getting the girls settled down after the picnic. Even after their baths, they were trying every trick in the book to keep from going to bed. Shaw hadn't been much help. He'd chuckled at everything the girls had said and done, thoroughly amused at her attempts to bring order.

She pointed to the stairs, putting on her most stern mommy face. "Upstairs. Now. You've had a busy day."

Chrissy climbed down from the chair. "Misser Shaw has to come, too. Can he read to us?"

"Not tonight. Scoot."

"But he has to come hear our prayers." Natalie made her desires known by directing a smile at Shaw.

"That's up to him." She glanced at him only to see him stand and wink at her.

"I can't miss out on the prayers."

He was enjoying her battle way too much. Upstairs, Shaw leaned against the door frame while she settled the girls under the covers. She sat on the edge of the bed as two pairs of hands pressed together and eyes closed.

Natalie went first, thanking God for a fun day, her mom, her friends and her grandma in heaven. Chrissy began her simple prayer next, thanking the Almighty for her mommy, her sister and her swings. She added Beaux to the list and Gwen's boys.

"And please, God, thank you for our Daddy Shaw, and keep him with us forever so he doesn't have to go to heaven like our other daddy did."

Lainie's heart froze in shock. What had prompted her child to say such a thing? She could feel Shaw's tension from across the room. She stole a glance. His jaw was flexing, his eyes dark as midnight, his forehead deeply creased. He pushed away from the door, his quick footsteps sounding on the stairs as he hurried away.

After kissing the girls good-night, Lainie sought the quiet of her bedroom. Never in her wildest dreams had she imagined that Chrissy had become so attached to Shaw, but she should have known. She had welcomed Shaw's presence in their lives as a positive role model, but she hadn't considered the eventual outcome.

Lainie sat in the upholstered chair, drawing her feet up. Shaw had looked horrified at her daughter's comment. Surely, he understood Chrissy was only four and didn't understand about having a daddy.

She debated whether to go and speak with him but decided against it. He'd made his position clear. His reaction told her everything she needed to know. Shaw wasn't the least bit interested in any kind of future, especially one that included another man's kids.

Shame on her for thinking otherwise. Shame on her again for entertaining thoughts of a different life. She'd come this far with just her girls, she could continue the same way. She'd allowed his attention, and mainly his kiss to cloud her common sense and capture her heart.

And he had. She was in love with Shaw. The last man she should ever care for. A man who had no interest in family and was content to be alone.

Shaw stood in his bedroom, one hand rubbing his jaw, a two-ton weight pressing on his chest, and a tornado of emotion roaring through his mind. *"Our Daddy Shaw."* Why had Chrissy said that? Did she think he was going to be her daddy?

A primal need to flee had yanked him from the room

and sent him running for his life. He wasn't ready for that. He adored those girls, but he'd never thought of himself as a daddy. Ever.

He'd been falling for Lainie from the first day he'd seen her so worried and vulnerable in the police station. He'd tried to resist the pull, but the more he was around her, the harder it had become. The first kiss had been to satisfy his curiosity. He'd figured that would end his obsession. But the kiss today had shifted his foundation. Chrissy had smashed it to pieces.

Frustrated and confused, he took a hot shower, hoping to calm his turmoil, but Chrissy's words refused to leave his mind. It wasn't just about his feelings for Lainie. The girls were part of the package, too. Together they were a huge responsibility. One he didn't know if he was capable of assuming. The girls saw their father as a superhero. He could never measure up.

Lainie had called him an honorable man. But there was nothing honorable about his behavior today. He'd crossed a line when he'd kissed her and taken a step in a direction he wasn't sure he could go. Beaux jumped up on the bed and laid his head on Shaw's chest, his black eyes staring sympathetically. "Pal, we're hip-deep in alligators and no way to drain the swamp."

There was only one way to proceed. He would stick with his commitment. He'd told Lainie he would take care of things until the library was complete. He'd keep his word. After that, he'd see what the Lord had in mind—if anything.

When his cell phone rang, he welcomed the interruption. But the late-night call brought bad news.

Shaw tossed his phone onto the bed, raking his fingers through his hair, trying to manage his anger and frustration. A sprinkler at the library had malfunctioned, and the company had notified the mayor, who had called Shaw. According to the report, there was two inches of water on the lower level.

The implications were gut-wrenching. Water could destroy all of the work they'd accomplished over the past weeks—wood floors, carpet, the new shelving. A knot the size of a basketball lodged in his stomach and refused to budge. He didn't want to think about the far-reaching ramifications. What if he lost his business? What if Dover lost its library? It would be his fault.

He shoved those concerns to the back of his mind. One thing at a time. He'd told the mayor he'd be right over, but first, he had someone else to share his bad news with. Lainie. She would be crushed. He'd considered waiting until after he'd seen the damage, but she'd hear his truck when he pulled out, and she'd worry.

Resting his hands on his hips, he set his jaw and prayed for strength. He pulled on his jeans and a shirt before picking up his cell again and dialing Lainie's number. She slept with the phone beside her. He hoped she was still awake. When she answered, he simply asked her to meet him at her back door.

His feet moved as if made of lead. His heart likewise. She was waiting for him when he arrived. He wished he could wait until morning, but he needed to get to the library and deal with the disaster. He had no idea when he'd get home again.

The fear in her eyes twisted his heart, but the sight of her smoothed the sharp edges of his emotions. Her hair was sleep-tousled, framing her face in delicate wisps. She clutched a robe closed at her throat. She looked beautiful. He forced his thoughts back to the problem at hand.

"Shaw. What's wrong?"

"One of the sprinkler heads failed at the library and flooded the first floor."

Her eyes widened in shock. "Oh, no. How bad?"

"Bad. I'll know more when I get there."

The worry in her eyes ripped through his heart. They were both thinking the same thing. This setback most likely meant they'd miss the deadline, and that would put them both out of work.

As he drove to the library, Shaw bore the weight of two worlds on his shoulders. Everything looked normal from the outside. But the flashing lights of a police cruiser and the mayor's large SUV told the real story. He also recognized the truck belonging to the owner of the sprinkler company. He braced himself for the worst.

Mayor Ogden charged toward him the moment he got out of the truck. "How could you let this happen? We're already weeks behind schedule. I'm beginning to think you aren't capable of handling this project. Do you realize the deadline is only eight days away? How long will it take to clean up this mess?"

Shaw strode toward the rear entrance of the library, dreading what he might find. "I won't know until I see how bad it is."

"Bad. Real bad." The mayor followed him. "This is all your fault."

"No, sir. This is the fault of the company who installed the system."

"Which you approved."

Shaw stepped into the building, his boots splashing through the accumulated water. It wasn't as bad as he'd expected. Definitely not two inches of water, but enough to ruin carpet and warp floors and baseboard. It could have been much worse. The broken sprinkler head had failed from the bottom and sent water directly downward. If it had sprayed outward the way it was designed to do, the walls would have been ruined, as well.

"I brought our shop vacs and fans, but we'll need more."

Shaw spun around to find Russ setting a large shop vacuum on the floor. "What are you doing here? Is Viola okay?"

"She's fine. Still waiting on a few test results, but right now they think it was an arthritis infection."

"I've never heard of that."

"Me, neither. But she's doing better. I figured you'd need extra help to get this cleaned up."

Just knowing Russ was with him took a huge load off his shoulders. "Well, I'm not going to send you home."

Russ chuckled. "Didn't figure you would."

Setting his mind to the task, Shaw made the necessary calls, then turned on the other shop vacuum and got to work.

It was after one in the morning when he and Russ called it a night. They'd done all they could for the moment, setting up the fans to run through the night to speed the drying process. Tomorrow, the professional cleaners would arrive and do their work, then he could make a better assessment of the damage.

By the time he returned to the house, his hopes for completing the project on time were in doubt. As he neared the back door, he saw lights in Lainie's kitchen. Was she waiting up for him? He hoped so. She appeared at the door, a small smile on her face as she pushed it open.

"I have fresh coffee or sweet tea if you'd rather have that."

"Tea sounds good. It was hot over there."

He sat at the table taking a long drink from the glass. Lainie sat beside him studying him with her expressive brown eyes. She was worried, anxious to hear the extent of the damage. "You want the good news first or the bad news?"

"The good."

He smiled. He knew she would say that. "Only the lower level was flooded. The second floor is untouched. The bad news—we can't tell the extent of the damage until we get the place dried out. The carpets in the reading room and the children's area are ruined. I think the wood floors will be okay if we can get them dried out quickly. A few of the shelves and cabinets have water damage, but we don't know how much yet." He met her gaze. It was nice to have someone to talk to and share his concerns.

Shaw enfolded her hands in his, finding comfort in the softness and the connection. "I have a bad feeling, Lainie. On the surface, it doesn't look too bad, but water can seep into everything, and it'll take days for everything to dry."

"There's nothing you can do in the meantime?"

"We'll pull out the carpet tomorrow and order a new one, but other than that, no." He let go of her hands. "I should have checked things again."

"This isn't your fault."

"Mayor Ogden wouldn't agree with you. He was waiting when I arrived, and he was demanding answers." Shaw ran a hand down the back of his neck. "Whatever the cause, the buck stops with me, Lainie.

As the contractor, I'm responsible for everything that happens. And I take those responsibilities seriously. If something or someone comes under my care, I'm not going to back out when things get difficult or inconvenient."

A cloud passed over Lainie's eyes. "And what about me and the girls? Are we your responsibility, too?"

"Of course. You had no one else. I had to make sure you were taken care of. I couldn't let you go to a shelter or sleep in your car. I promised you I'd take care of things until the library was done and you could go to work. I keep my promises."

Lainie picked up his empty glass and carried it to the sink. "It's all about responsibility, isn't it?"

"Yes." Something in Lainie's attitude had changed, but he didn't have the strength to analyze it at the moment. He was tired, and a headache like a nail gun was shooting pains through his skull. He needed sleep. Tomorrow was going to be a nightmare.

He stood and moved to the door. "Thanks for waiting up and for the tea. Don't worry. I'll get it all taken care of."

Lainie crossed her arms over her chest, her mouth set in a thin line, her usually warm brown eyes dark and hard. "I'm sure you will. You'd better go. You have a lot of responsibility to take care of."

Shaw searched her face for some explanation. Why had she turned so cold? What had he said that had angered her? "Lainie?"

"You'd better go."

Too tired to argue, he walked out. Whatever was bothering her would have to wait.

Chapter Eleven

Lainie leaned back in her chair, gently stretching her arm back and forth to exercise the muscles the way the therapist had taught her. Her elbow was getting better, but she had to be careful not to spend too much time at the keyboard. It had been three days since the flood, and everyone was pushing themselves to the limits to make repairs and get things back on track. She hadn't seen Shaw since the night he had returned from the library.

"If the books had been in place when the sprinkler broke, we'd have lost them, too." Millie sealed up a box, adding a firm slap to the top. "Another one done."

Lainie glanced up from her computer. "It feels like we're buried in boxes. First they come in, we empty them, sort them, then box them back up again. This would be so much simpler if we were in the library already. We could place them right on the shelves."

Millie sat beside her. "I hate to admit it, but this is more work than I expected. Maybe the board is right. I *am* too old to handle this job."

Lainie squeezed her friend's hand. "Not true. You

could have done it easily. This was a huge job. Anyone would be worn-out."

"Not you. You're like the little engine that could. Working here all day, doing Shaw's bookkeeping at night and taking care of your girls. You're going to be a blessing to this town, Lainie."

"Thank you. That means a lot. I hope I get the chance to prove you right." She glanced out the small carriage house windows toward the large mansion. "I'm worried. Shaw is so discouraged. I'm afraid the damage is worse than he's letting on."

"Really? Russ told me things were looking good, and they should be done for the big inspection." Millie studied her from over the rim of her glasses. "Maybe something else is bothering Shaw. Something personal. Maybe the same thing that's bothering you?"

"The only thing bothering me is impatience. I want this library open so I can start work." Millie sent her a skeptical grin and went back to packing. Lainie's gaze drifted out the window to the library again. Shaw and his crew had pulled up the carpet the other day and hauled off some of the shelves and cabinets that needed repair. After they'd left, she'd gathered her courage and peeked inside the old mansion. Even with the surfaces dried out, the stench from wet carpet, damp wood and concrete permeated the air. She'd managed to get into the reception area and survey the damage. The large industrial fans were still blowing, making a racket, but to her untrained eye, it looked hopeless.

She thought about all the work Shaw and his men had put into the building—the hours, the skill and dedication—and her eyes burned. He would be heartbroken. He took pride in his work. He wanted the library for the town, but he needed it for his future, too. So did she. The deadline was Monday, less than four days away. She didn't see any way the library could open on schedule and still have time to bring in the furniture and all the books.

When Lainie arrived home that evening, she was exhausted. She picked up the girls from Gwen's, fed them and sent them out to play until bath time. She needed a few minutes to unwind. Shaw wasn't home. She knew he'd work through the night to get finished. He had to be exhausted, too. She was starting to worry about him.

On the front porch, she pulled the mail from her box and Shaw's, sorting through it as she went back inside. She placed his on the small table in the main hall, then went into her duplex. Her mail consisted of two bills she'd had forwarded and one official-looking envelope. It was addressed to Mrs. Craig Hollings. The bold return address was from a detective agency.

Icy fear twisted around her heart. Her fingers trembled as she opened the seal on the thin paper. Her eyes scanned the contents, but her brain struggled to process the words. She forced herself to take a calming breath before starting again.

Craig's mother had tracked her down and she was coming to Dover to meet with her. The rest of the words on the paper blurred. All the horrible things Craig had warned her about burst forth, releasing her darkest fears. He'd always said his parents would try to break up their marriage if they found them, and push for custody of any children they had. Their controlling behavior was one of the reasons he'd cut all ties with them.

Was his mother coming to try and take the girls away? What if Lainie had to go to court? How would she afford to fight for them? She was a good mother. No court in the land would take them away. But what if they did? A wave of panic bent her forward and she clutched her stomach.

Throat pinched with fear, Lainie grabbed her cell and called Shaw. It didn't occur to her until he answered that there was nothing he could do to help. But hearing his voice immediately eased her fears, giving her a sense of calm and support to cling to. "Shaw, how soon are you coming home?"

"Not for a few more hours. What's wrong? You sound upset."

"I received a letter from my mother-in-law today. She's coming to Dover."

"How did she find you?"

Lainie stared at the letter in her hand trying to keep her senses. "She hired a detective agency."

"Did she say why she was coming?"

"No. Maybe." She couldn't think straight. "She said she wanted to meet to discuss family issues." Lainie paced the room, gripping the phone like a lifeline. "What if she's coming to check me out to see if I'm a good mother? Craig warned me she'd be ruthless if she ever found out about me."

"I'll be right there."

The minutes crawled by as she waited for Shaw. Her stomach was churning. Fear had coated her skin with dampness. She couldn't concentrate. She prayed constantly, but even that failed to calm her anxiety. She let the girls play outside longer than usual, not wanting them to see her so upset.

She handed Shaw the letter the moment he stepped

inside the kitchen, chewing her thumbnail nervously as she waited for him to read it.

"What do you think she wants?"

"Maybe exactly what she says. To meet and discuss family issues."

"What issues? Does she want to take my girls?"

Shaw slipped an arm around her shoulders. "Don't jump to conclusions, Lainie. It might mean nothing at all."

She allowed her head to rest on his shoulder a moment before pulling away. "No. It means something. Craig rarely talked about his parents, but when he did, he said horrible things about them. He said they lied to him, that they'd want to take the baby if they knew about her." She wrapped her arms around her waist. "I thought I'd hear from them after his death, but when I didn't, I assumed they didn't care. As the years passed, I forgot about them. Now, out of the blue, she shows up. What does she want? Why now after all this time?"

"What can I do? Just tell me."

"I don't know. I want to grab my girls and run, but I know that's ridiculous. But if she wants to fight for them, I can't afford a court battle."

"Lainie, you're getting upset before you know the situation." He pulled her into his arms. "I'll be here beside you. Let's hear what she wants first before we second-guess her motives."

The letter had shattered her common sense. Her deep fear of losing her girls raged through her like a volcanic explosion. Lainie clung to him, needing the comfort he offered. "I have to be prepared. I have to be ready to show her I'm a good mother and I can provide for them, that I have a job—" She stilled. "Oh, Shaw, I might not have a job if the library doesn't get done."

"It will."

"But what if it doesn't? The flood could ruin the whole thing." She pulled away, placing her hands on her cheeks as she saw her life from her mother-in-law's perspective. "It all looks so bad right now. The town doesn't want me here, the library might not be done and I'll be unemployed. I'm living in the home of the town's most notorious bachelor, accepting gifts of money from him. It's a scene right out of a bad soap opera."

Shaw smiled. "I don't think I'm notorious. And you're my tenant."

She glared. "You know what I mean. My whole life right now looks shady. And we don't even have a lease to show her."

"I'll draw one up. Tell me what you need me to do. I'll do whatever you want. I won't let her take the girls from you."

"You don't have any say in the matter."

"But I have friends who can help. Some with powerful influence."

Lainie shook her head, trying to think around the fear scraping every nerve raw. "I need to look in charge and competent. That I am providing the best loving environment for them. When I told Mrs. Forsythe what Craig had said about his parents, she suggested I get married again. Then there would be no way she could take the girls away."

Shaw set his hands on his hips. "That's an idea. If she questions your reputation, tell her we're engaged. If she thinks you're involved with someone able to provide a solid home, she won't do anything."

It was a silly idea, but Lainie was frantic, and at the moment, any idea was worth considering. She pressed her fingers to her temples. She had to get a grip. Shaw was right. She was panicking over something she didn't know would happen. "No. Thanks, Shaw, but no one would believe you're in love with me." She looked into his eyes and thought she saw a flash of pain behind the dark blue. The notion sent a wave of longing zipping through her body. For a second, she let herself believe he did love her. But then she remembered he was a happy bachelor, and merely saw her and the girls as his obligation.

Shaw frowned. "Why not?"

"Dover's most eligible single man and a mom with two kids. You said it yourself. You're not the marrying kind."

"Maybe I've changed my mind."

Lainie didn't want to think about what he might mean. "I don't think this woman will be easily fooled. I'm afraid the only way to convince her would be to produce a marriage license."

"Then let's show her proof. Marry me."

Her heart stopped before kicking into action again. He couldn't be serious. He was taking his responsibility to the extreme. "Don't be ridiculous. I'd do anything to protect my girls, but I stop short of marrying a man who—" The words *doesn't love me* died on her lips. She swallowed and turned away. Oh, but how she wished he did.

"Lainie, it wouldn't be real. I have a good friend at the courthouse. All we need is a piece of paper that shows we're serious. I can get a marriage application or even a license. It won't be legit, but it will look official to her."

At her wit's end, Lainie had to admit it wasn't a bad idea. If Craig's mother questioned her current situation, she would produce Shaw and the license. There would be nothing the woman could do.

"All right," she said. "But just as a last resort." Drained from worry and fear, Lainie sank onto a kitchen chair.

Shaw rested his hand on her arm. "Lainie, it'll be all right. You're scared and worn down from all the stress of the library. You're not thinking clearly. I'll be with you. Whatever she throws at us, we'll tackle it together."

"This isn't your fight, but thank you. I couldn't have handled any of this without you."

"Nonsense. No one is more capable and determined than you. Or more beautiful."

Lainie laughed, wiping the tears from her face. "Oh, right. Red eyed and weepy."

"That's the way you looked when I first saw you in the station. I thought the same thing then." He touched her chin with his fingertips, his blue eyes intense and probing. "I told you I'd take care of you."

His words pierced her heart, adding another pain to her already-tattered emotions. He hadn't said he loved her. The girls scrambled in the door, shattering the moment.

"Mommy, we're thirsty."

She hid her hurt in the activity of fixing drinks, aware of Shaw moving toward the door.

"I'd better get back. We'll talk more later. Don't worry about anything."

She nodded, afraid of speaking and losing control of

her emotions. She made the girls a quick supper, keeping busy with getting her daughters ready for bed. Once again, Shaw had stepped in to fix her life and handle her problems. She didn't want him to fix her life. She wanted him to care for her. Not because he felt obligated, but because he loved her.

Right now she needed to get prepared to meet her mother-in-law. But worrying didn't solve anything. She'd do her part to make sure the library was done and trust that Shaw would keep his word to her and the town and meet the deadline.

Lainie scanned the bar code on the plastic library card then typed in the information written on the application. She'd wanted to have all the cards ready to hand out on opening day, but that was in three days, and she was behind. She'd decided to get the books ready before the cards. Of course, she was having trouble concentrating on anything since the letter had arrived from her mother-in-law yesterday.

The message had said she'd arrive sometime this week. The worst possible week to show up. Shaw was working like a madman trying to finish the last details on the library. She and Millie were trying to process and organize as many of the books as possible, but there were still far too many boxes sitting in Dutch's warehouse. Along with chairs, tables, benches plus beanbags for the kids to sit on.

The tech guys were installing the computers today, but she still couldn't start moving the books in until that final inspection was completed. Shaw had scheduled it for tomorrow.

She sighed and brushed her hair off her face. Her

stomach was in knots, and she'd been unable to eat since the letter had arrived. She felt as if she was about to explode from the stress. It was near noon when she looked up to see Shaw coming in the door. The sight of him eased her tension. He had that effect on her.

He stopped at the worktable, pulling an envelope from his shirt pocket. "I have our marriage license."

An odd rush of excitement made her light-headed. She stood, removing the paper from the envelope and studied it. Seeing their names on a very official-looking marriage license caused an odd tightness in her throat. "It looks real."

"It is. The document, I mean. It wouldn't be honored if we presented it at the courthouse, but it's on official paper."

"Do I want to know how you did this?"

"Nothing illegal, I promise."

Lainie prayed the ruse would convince her mother-in-law that she and Shaw were serious and able to provide a stable home for the girls. A wave of fear increased her heart rate. She pressed her hands to her face. "Oh, Shaw! What if she wants to take my girls?"

He pulled her against his chest. "I won't let anyone take those girls from you. I promise."

She wiggled out of his arms. No need to torment herself with something that couldn't be. "I'm sorry. You have enough on your plate without worrying about my problems."

"We're getting close. Everything should be done for the inspection tomorrow. Let's pray the inspector shows up on time."

"This is nerve-racking. I can feel the clock ticking

in the back of my mind. One for the library and one for my future."

"Hang in there." He held up the envelope, smiling confidently. "We have some ammunition."

His plan was outrageous, and she should never have agreed to it. "Don't take this the wrong way, but I hope we don't have to use that."

"Right. Me, too. We'll wait and see what she wants before we produce our evidence."

Friday afternoon slipped away, adding further to Lainie's frustration. She'd planned on going to Dutch's warehouse to check on the shipments of furniture that had been arriving. She needed to make sure each piece was what she'd ordered, but there hadn't been time. Between her injured arm and the flood, she'd fallen over a week behind. She was trusting that none of the deliveries were wrong.

She and Millie had decided they'd make do as best they could. The library was required to have furniture and books in place. Blake had checked, and nothing in the specifications mentioned anything about being completely furnished and stocked. Thank God for loopholes.

Still, there was so much to do in only two days, and she was beginning to lose hope. She kept up a confident face for Millie and Shaw, but inside, her heart was breaking. She didn't see any way it would happen.

The last thing she needed was a visit from her mother-in-law. In her present state of mind, Lainie wasn't sure she could maintain a civil attitude with the woman.

Millie joined her at the computer. "How's it going?" She looked at the box of newly scanned library cards, then flipped the edges of the stack of applications still waiting to be entered into the computer. "You want me to do this for a while? I'm waiting for Dutch to bring a few more boxes."

Lainie opened her mouth to reply when her cell rang. She scooped it up, her heart turning to ice when she saw the name Hollingsworth. Craig's real last name. Her mother-in-law was here. Paralyzed with fear, she stared at the name. Her whole life could change with this one call. She pushed the button and muttered a soft hello. She closed her eyes as the voice on the other end spoke. Heart pounding, she kept her responses short. Her hand trembled as she ended the call.

"Well?" Millie asked. "Was that her?"

"She's coming by this evening. What if she wants to take my children away?"

"Don't go borrowing trouble. Didn't Shaw say he'd be with you when you met her?"

She nodded, pacing the small work area. She wasn't sure she wanted Shaw with her now. She'd become too dependent on him, too quick to turn to him to fix things. She needed to face this woman on her own and let her know she was willing to fight for her family no matter what. If things became contentious, she'd call Shaw, and they'd present the evidence of their intentions. And dare her to challenge it.

"I've got to go." She grabbed her purse and headed out. She pulled into the driveway at home with no recollection of having driven there. Inside, she flitted from one task to the next. Straightening the kitchen, checking her makeup, wondering whether to leave the girls at Gwen's while the woman was here or have them with her. What was the right thing to do?

She picked up her cell to call Shaw and let him know, only to put it down again. She could do this. She was grateful for his help and his crazy marriage license plan—though she still doubted it would work—but she had to do this alone. She would show Mrs. Hollingsworth she was a strong, capable woman who wasn't easily intimidated, and who could handle anything life threw at her. But what she really wanted was to call Shaw and have him come and hold her and assure her everything would be all right.

Her gaze landed on her Bible lying open on the kitchen table. But it wasn't Shaw's strength she should be seeking. Sinking onto the chair, she clasped her hands and bowed her head. *Forgive me Father for my fear and doubt. For borrowing trouble. I am a good mother, a woman of faith. Give me courage and strength to face this woman. I know You'll work it out for good.*

The fear eased as she prayed, and her courage grew. She made her decision. She would bring the girls home from Gwen's, tell them a little about their visitor, then face whatever was to come.

A short while later, Lainie was prepared. The girls were playing in the Princess Club, the house was straightened and everyone was presentable. There was nothing more she could do. According to the clock, Mrs. Hollingsworth should be arriving any minute. Panic rose and clogged her throat, flooding her mind. She couldn't do this alone. She couldn't. Grabbing her phone, she dialed Shaw's number, gasping small breaths of air as she waited. Why didn't he answer? She heard the click in her ear and didn't wait for him to speak.

"She's here. She'll be at the house any second now."

"Why didn't you call me?"

"I thought I could do it alone, but I'm scared."

"It'll be okay. Stay calm. I'm in Sawyer's Bend. I had to pick up some hardware. I'm on my way. Stall her as best you can."

Lainie hung up the phone, feeling abandoned and defeated. Sawyer's Bend. It would take him twenty minutes or more to get here. *Lord forgive me for being so weak.*

Opening her apartment door, she stepped into the hall to watch out the front door for her mother-in-law's arrival. The silver car pulled to a stop at the curb in the front of the house. A woman got out and started up the sidewalk. Through the leaded glass panes, it was impossible to see what she looked like. With one more heartfelt prayer, Lainie opened the door at the first knock.

The woman she saw was nothing like what she'd expected. She'd envisioned Craig's mother as tall and thin with a superior glare and impeccably groomed. But this woman was medium height, slightly plump, with gray hair and a pleasant face.

Lainie cleared her throat. "Mrs. Hollingsworth. Won't you come in?"

"Thank you." She stepped into the foyer and glanced around, her expression puzzled.

Lainie squelched the urge to explain about the old house. She motioned her toward the door on her side of the house.

Mrs. Hollingsworth stopped inside the living room and faced her. "You're Lainie? My son's wife."

"Yes."

"You're not what I expected." She raised her hand. "That came out wrong. I had formed a picture of you in my mind as cool and aloof, but I can see you're nothing like that."

Lainie wasn't sure what to make of her comment. "Won't you sit down?"

"Mommy?"

She'd almost forgotten about the girls. "Mrs. Hollingsworth, these are my daughters, Natalie and Chrissy."

Mrs. Hollingsworth's eyes grew moist. "Hello. I've waited a long time to meet you."

The girls eyed the woman suspiciously, staying close to Lainie's side. "Girls, go back and play while Mrs. Hollingsworth and I talk."

Once they were settled on the sofa, Lainie decided to take command. "I have a lot of questions, Mrs. Hollingsworth. The main one being, what do you want here?"

"I wanted to meet my grandchildren and my daughter-in-law."

"Is that all? Because if you've come to try and take my girls away, I will fight you with everything I have."

Mrs. Hollingsworth's face pressed into a deep frown. "I have no desire to do that. Whatever gave you such an idea?"

"Craig. He said if you ever tracked him down, and found out about our children, you'd stop at nothing to get them."

Her mother-in-law hastily pulled a tissue from her purse and dabbed at her eyes. "I was afraid this might happen, but I'd hoped…" She composed herself. "What did my son tell you about his father and me?"

Her husband's warnings echoed inside her head, but she was finding it hard to apply them to this woman. "That you lied to him. That he cut all ties and never wanted to have anything to do with you. That's why he changed his name. He didn't want you to track him down and force yourselves into our lives. He would get very angry when he spoke of you, though he mentioned you only a couple times when we were married."

Mrs. Hollingsworth nodded, her hands twisting the tissue into knots. "I'd hoped he'd come to understand. But I think I knew when I learned he'd changed his name he would never forgive us." She glanced at the girls before going on. "My husband and I couldn't have children so we adopted Craig when he was three months old. We adored him and probably spoiled him more than we should have. We always planned to tell him he was adopted, but the time was never right and the years passed. When he graduated from high school, we realized we needed to let him know. He didn't take it well. He was furious. We tried to explain, but he was so angry. He said some horrible things to us, and then he left. We tried to find him, but we couldn't keep track. We finally gave up, hoping someday he would come to understand."

"I had no idea. He never said anything." Lainie could easily see her husband holding a grudge. He harbored resentment too long. "How did you find us?"

"From time to time, we'd hire a detective to search for him. One of them discovered he'd changed his name. It helped narrow the search." She smiled. "I'm so glad to have found you. You're lovely. I'm sure my son loved you very much."

"He did. And his daughter. Chrissy was born after the accident."

Mrs. Hollingsworth looked over at the girls playing in the corner. "They are so beautiful. I didn't come here to disrupt your life, only to find you, and ask if perhaps

I could come and see you and the children occasionally. They look so much like their father."

"Yes, they do." Lainie's fears melted away. Mrs. Hollingsworth was a mother looking to reconnect with her son, and find answers and closure. She understood those things. She'd looked for them as she'd grieved. It would be nice to have a grandmother for the girls.

The familiar rumble of Shaw's truck sounded as he pulled into the driveway. He was coming to rescue her. But she didn't need him to. She had to stop him before he charged in thinking he was saving the day. Their plan would only create confusion and suspicion now.

"Mrs. Hollingsworth, I need to speak to my landlord a moment. If you'll excuse me. Girls, why don't you show Mrs.—" she glanced at the woman and saw hope in her blue eyes "—your grandmother the Princess Club."

Natalie frowned. "I thought our grandma was in heaven."

"That was Grandma Denton. My mother. This is your daddy's mother."

Natalie smiled. "I always wanted a grandma."

Lainie hurried to the back porch, stopping Shaw as he topped the steps. He grasped her arms, his face filled with concern. "Are you all right? Has she threatened you?"

She placed her hands on his chest. His heart was beating wildly. "No. It's all right. She's a sweet lady and she has no intention of taking my girls."

"What?"

"I can't explain right now. But it's okay. You can go back to the library. I don't need you, after all." She pushed away, but Shaw took her arm and stopped her.

"I don't understand."

"I'll tell you all about it later. Promise."

Lainie hurried back inside, pausing when she saw her daughters. Mrs. Hollingsworth had pulled up a chair near their little table, and was enjoying a cup of "tea." The joy on the three faces chased away the last of her fears. Smiling, she joined her family in the Princess Club.

Shaw stood on the back porch, feeling as if he'd been sucker punched. Lainie didn't need him. He'd rushed in like a white knight only to be told he wasn't wanted. She didn't want help from a man who had made her a widow. She hadn't voiced the words the other day, but he knew what she'd meant to say. He stared at his back door, not knowing whether to go inside or go back to the library. Slowly, he pivoted and headed back to his truck. He was needed at the library. There was still a lot to do before the inspector came. He'd got word from the mayor that the benefactor's representative would be in town in the morning to conduct their own inspection to make sure all points in the bequest had been met.

Inside his cab, he inserted the key in the ignition, then leaned back against the seat. He had a lot of unanswered questions where Lainie and her mother-in-law were concerned, but all that should matter was that the woman wasn't going to try and take Natalie and Chrissy away. Lainie seemed happy, even relaxed. Whatever had happened was a good thing.

So why did he feel so miserable? Lainie was safe, and she'd connected with Craig's family. Shaw could rest easy. He didn't have to be responsible for them any longer. His ego was bruised—that was all. He had arrived, had charged in to save the day and had been dismissed.

"I don't need you." Her words pierced deep into his heart. She was turning away from him. Like his mother had. Like Vicki had. He should have expected this. It was the pattern of all his relationships. So why was this time harder than the others? His heart was being shredded into tiny pieces. His blood surged through his veins like they were on fire. His chest was cold and tight, each breath painful.

He pulled the envelope from his pocket and removed the license. It was a joke. A stupid plan that hadn't been needed. It probably wouldn't have worked anyway. Now he could go back to his single life, his job and look to the future.

His gaze rested on the names typed onto the marriage license. Alaine Denton Hollings and Goudchaux Anthony McKinney. It wasn't real. But suddenly he wished with all his heart it was.

The truth stole what little breath was left in his chest. He loved Lainie more than anything on earth. He wanted to be married to her, to take care of her for the rest of his life, to cherish her and her precious children.

His heart swelled, threatening to burst his ribs. Like a cloud lifting from his mind, he understood what others talked about—loving completely, wholly. Vicki said if he met the right person, he'd be able to remove the lock on his heart, the place where he'd sealed up his love for fear of being hurt again. Now he had no fear, no doubts and no questions. Only the knowledge that he wanted to spend the rest of his life with Lainie. He wanted to be there to fix all her problems, to hold her hand when she was scared, to fight the monsters and slay the dragons.

Somehow, Lainie and her girls had picked the lock on his heart, one tumbler at a time, and set him free. Another truth reared its head, one that darkened his joy. He had fallen in love with Lainie, but it was too late. He wasn't sure what had happened between her and the mother-in-law, but it had changed things. She had a new future, and he doubted there was any room for him in it.

He'd waited too long, held on to his fear too tightly, and now he was paying the price. This was something he couldn't fix with a hammer and nail, or a favor called in. All that was left to do was finish the library, salvage his company and make sure Lainie had a job.

That's all he could do.

Chapter Twelve

It was late afternoon on Saturday before Lainie found a moment to sit and catch her breath. She and Millie were trying to get as much done today as possible. The final inspection on the construction was due to take place shortly and they were praying everything would pass. The deadline was Monday. Lainie tried not to think about the massive task ahead.

"Your mother-in-law sounds like a very sweet lady." Millie smiled over the computer screen where she was entering library card information.

Lainie nodded. "She is. The girls are so excited to have a grandma. She wants us to come down to New Orleans to meet the grandfather. He's a teacher. She works at a bank."

"How did Shaw take the news?"

She shrugged. "I told him everything was okay, but I haven't had a chance to talk to him today. We're both too busy."

"I'm sure he's happy for you."

Millie's tone suggested otherwise. A jolt of concern

shot through Lainie's heart. "Is something wrong with him? Is he okay?"

"Depends on what you mean by *okay.*"

"Millie, I don't have time for twenty questions."

"All right." Millie placed her hands on the arm of the chair and peered at her. "The man's in love with you."

Lainie's heart skipped a beat. "He's just a friend. He's told me a dozen times he's not going to give up his bachelor life."

"He would for you and your girls."

"Did he tell you that?"

"He didn't have to. He's loved you for a long time. I just don't think he knew it himself until recently."

"That doesn't make sense. Nothing has changed."

Millie crossed her arms over her chest, a frown on her face. "Something has. He's like a lost puppy today."

The carriage house door opened and the subject of their discussion stepped in. "Good afternoon. I just wanted to deliver some good news."

He looked wonderful. The dark jeans he wore made him seem taller and the white polo shirt with the Mc-Kinney Construction logo brought out his deep blue eyes. Lainie smiled at him, but he kept his gaze on Millie.

"The city inspector has given us the green light to occupy the building."

"And the representative from the donor?" Millie asked.

"Got the okay from him, as well. That gives us two days to get as much moved into the rooms as possible."

Lainie's throat contracted with disappointment. She might as well have been invisible. Shaw was directing all his comments to Millie and completely ignoring her.

A frown appeared on Millie's forehead. "Do you think we can get all the books and furniture moved in time?"

Shaw nodded. "It'll take some doing, but yes. I think we can."

He sounded confident, but she could see he was worried. It was a massive job. Thousands of books, hundreds of boxes and a warehouse full of furniture.

"I've got a few papers to sign first, but we can start hauling books right away."

Shaw left without a backward glance in her direction. Her heart beat faster. Was Millie right? She'd kept her own feelings to herself for fear of damaging their friendship. Maybe she should have spoken up. But she'd deal with Shaw later. Right now they had to get busy.

Sunday morning, Lainie was tempted to skip church to go to the library, but then she thought about how the Lord had worked everything out, and she knew she couldn't go to the library until she thanked Him with praise and worship. He'd blessed her far more than she'd ever imagined.

They attended the early service, then hurried home and changed into work clothes. She didn't like working on the Sabbath, but with the deadline looming, they needed every minute they could find. Mrs. Hollingsworth—Irene—had offered to watch the girls today, and Lainie had happily accepted. The four of them had bonded quickly, giving Lainie the sense of family she'd missed for so long.

"Are you sure you'll be okay, Irene? I have no idea when I'll be home."

"We'll be fine." Irene hugged Natalie to her side. Chrissy waved goodbye from across the table.

"Call me if you need anything. Gwen will be next door if you need her."

Irene waved her away. "Go. Make your deadline."

Lainie drove the backstreet shortcut to the library to save time. A block from the library, she got stuck in a line of cars moving at a snail's pace. As she eased around the corner, she noticed the street in front of the library was lined with vehicles. Dozens of people stood on the front lawn. Three large trucks were parked in the driveway.

She was forced to pull around to the next block before finding a place to park. She dashed back to the library, her mind conjuring all kinds of disasters that might have occurred overnight to threaten the deadline once again. She found Millie standing near the carriage house, tears streaming down her face. "What's wrong? What's happened?"

Millie pulled her into a tight embrace. "It's an answer to our prayers. All these people, these trucks, they're here to help us move everything into the library."

Lainie stared at the crowd, recognizing a few faces here and there. Gwen's mother, Mrs. Adams; Blake Prescott. "Millie, did you arrange this?"

"No, dear. I haven't had time to do much of anything. Everyone showed up asking how they could help."

A swell of joy and gratitude stole her breath, bringing tears to her eyes. This is what she'd come to a small town for. This was the dream she'd cherished from childhood. Being part of a community that cared and helped each other when needed.

She saw Shaw strolling toward her through the

crowd. The sight of him filled her with happiness. He walked with that confident swagger she'd come to admire. His wide smile and flashing eyes made her insides feel as if they were dissolving into mush. But it was his tender heart that had won her over. He was a man who cared deeply for others. She loved him. Completely. Totally.

He stopped in front of her, holding her with his blue gaze. "I told you they'd come around. They're all here to help you."

"Not me. The library."

He touched her arm. Briefly. "You. I'm so proud of you. Your devotion to this building and your tenacity in making sure the books were ordered has endeared you to every person in Dover."

Tears streamed down her cheeks. Words failed her. People were smiling, waving at her and giving the thumbs-up sign. In this moment, she finally felt like she belonged. "I don't know what to say."

Shaw spread his arms. "Start giving orders. Tell us what to do so we can get this job rolling."

Lainie wiped her eyes, her mind already organizing what needed to be done. She thanked everyone, then started assigning tasks.

Shaw took charge of the people hauling boxes from Dutch's warehouse, while she and Millie stood in the middle of the library and directed each box to its proper location. For the rest of the day, a steady stream of people tramped through the Dover Public Library.

Many of the items weren't in the right place, none of the books had been shelved according to the Dewey decimal system, only by category, but the library was ready for business. The rest could be handled a little at a time while serving the residents of Dover.

It was dark when Lainie returned home. Irene had put the children to bed and was eager to get back to The Lady Banks Inn where she was staying. Lainie wanted to wait up to talk to Shaw. She still hadn't had time to fill him in on her situation with Irene, but she was exhausted and knew he was, too.

Beaux, who had been stretched out on her kitchen floor, rose and rubbed his jaw against her leg. That meant he was hungry. She scratched his ear. "Did anyone bother to feed you today?"

Motioning the dog to follow, she walked to Shaw's kitchen and filled Beaux's dish from the plastic container at the end of the counter. After filling his water dish, she started to leave, but something on the table caught her attention. She picked it up, unable to believe what she was seeing. The marriage license. Why did he still have it? Why hadn't he thrown it away? It was useless.

She read the names, hers and his. She allowed herself to believe it was real. That Millie was right and the bachelor loved her. But he didn't. Shaw wasn't ready to give up his single life, and she couldn't expect him, or any man, to take on the responsibility of her daughters.

But if any man could or would, she'd want it to be him.

Lainie stood in front of the mirror, adjusting her necklace over her coral blouse, unable to keep the smile from her face and the butterflies settled in her stomach. Today was the grand opening of the Dover Public Library, and her first official day as head librarian. Yesterday morning had welcomed another wave of vol-

unteers eager to help with the move. Lainie was hum-
bled again by the kindness of her new community. What
had started out so badly had ended up a blessing she
would cherish forever.

After sending the girls to Gwen's, she hurried to
the library. Millie had insisted they have a celebratory
opening day, and once again, Lainie was overwhelmed
by the generosity of the people of Dover. Petals and
Pails flower shop sent a large bouquet that graced the
table in the entrance. The Magnolia Café donated an
assortment of cookies and snacks, and Randall's grocery provided beverages. The Friends of the Library
were on hand to serve as hostesses and were signing
up more volunteers.

However, one person was noticeably absent. Shaw.

But then, what had she expected? His job was done.
He'd honored his contract and cemented his business
reputation. He had a successful future ahead, and she
was happy for him. But there was a giant hole in her
heart that he'd filled, and she knew no one else would
ever fit the spot.

Opening day was filled with challenges. Books were
hard to locate, the line to pick up library cards was too
long and two of the computers weren't working prop-
erly, but no one seemed to mind.

The day passed in a blur of activity, so Lainie was
surprised when Millie locked the front door, officially
ending The Dover Public Library's grand opening.

Millie wiped her brow. "I think we did well for our
first day."

Lainie chuckled. "I think we did a phenomenal job.
I just hope the interest will continue. I can't help think

about how libraries everywhere are struggling to stay relevant."

"I'm not worried. Once you get your new ideas up and running, you'll be busy every minute. Maybe now you can start living a more normal schedule."

"That would be nice. I feel like I've missed too much time with my girls as it is."

"Is your mother-in-law still here?"

"No. She had to go back to New Orleans, but she's invited us to visit soon and meet her husband."

"Why don't you go this weekend? Things will slow down over the next few days, and I can handle the library on Saturday." She grinned. "I've had some experience, you know."

"Oh, I don't know. It's such short notice for them."

"New Orleans is only an hour and a half away. Even if you went for the day, it would be a good break for you."

"I'll think about it."

The more Lainie considered Millie's idea, the more she liked it. It would be nice to get away from the constant worry about deadlines and take time to relax and enjoy her girls. Meeting their grandfather would be nice, too. Lainie felt sure he would be as warm as his wife. Time away from Shaw might be wise, also. She was torn between longing to be with him and determination to stay away. It was tearing her apart.

Her first order of business when she got back would be to find a new place to live. Coming to Dover had been a blessing, not only for her new job, but it had allowed her to let go of the past and move forward and heal the wounds with her in-laws.

But it hadn't won her the heart of the man she loved.

* * *

Shaw studied the blueprints on his desk, scribbling figures on a notepad. A new office building was going up near the municipal complex. It was a big job, but he felt certain he could put in a competitive bid. If he got this contract, McKinney Construction would be on solid footing for a long while. He'd chosen to work in his shop office today. With his other jobs back on track, it was time to start lining up new projects. But his thoughts kept straying to the library, and he wondered how Lainie was managing.

He sensed the moment when his foreman stopped in the doorway. He ignored him, hoping he'd go away.

"You want to tell me what's eating at you?"

Shaw set his jaw. No use trying to ignore Russ when he was curious. "Just trying to get a bid ready."

Russ chuckled softly. "Have you been by the library lately?"

He strived to keep his tone indifferent. "I stopped by the other day for a second. Just to see if everything was okay."

"Did you talk to her?"

No need to ask who "her" was. "No. She was busy, so—" He'd watched her from behind the shelves like a scared kid. She'd flitted around like a beautiful butterfly, smiling, happy. Her brown eyes had sparkled like stars, and her energy and joy had infected everyone near her. She'd been in her element.

"When are you going to tell her how you feel?"

Shaw shook his head, pretending to study the blueprints. "She has her dream. She doesn't need anything else."

"Did she say that?"

"Yes. She did."

"Do you love her?"

Shaw tossed his pencil down, planting his elbows on the desk and clasping his hands in front of his chin. He needed help sorting out his life. Might as well fess up. "Yes. I do, but I thought I loved Vicki, too, and it wasn't enough. What if I can't figure out what Lainie wants? What if I can't be the man she needs?"

Russ approached the desk, an understanding smile flashing in his dark face. "My Viola likes those musical shows. She'd go to the ball games with me even though she doesn't like 'em much. So I go to a few of those plays they have at Thalia Mara Hall. We saw one this past spring, and the words to one of the songs stuck with me. The guy wanted to know how to handle a woman, and the answer was to just love her. That's all. Love her."

It couldn't be that simple. "Is that how you've stayed married so long?"

"That, and a mutual faith and desire to make the other happy. My wife is the most important thing in my life, along with my kids. If I lost her, I'd lose everything." Russ gave him an encouraging pat on the back. "When the time comes, I'll give you all my secrets."

Was there a time for him? Would there ever be? What if Lainie was the one, and he had let her go because of his doubts? Vicki had been important to him, and her rejection had hurt, but losing her hadn't cost him anything except a bruised ego and dented pride. He'd picked up and gone on. He written off being jilted as a lesson learned, not the loss of a lifetime.

Shaw slipped out of the office and drove to the project on the opposite side of town—a sunroom addition so far behind schedule the owners had threatened to sue. He couldn't put them off any longer. With the library up and running, he could start taking on more projects. And restore his old Victorian and get it sold.

He couldn't stay there any longer. Too many memories. No little faces peeking through the French door, no front porch chair with Lainie curled up in the morning. No one to use the swings in the backyard. He'd take them down. It would hurt too much to see them every day.

The library was done. His obligation to Lainie was over and she would be moving out and getting on with her life. The thought was like a punch in the gut. He would lose her.

And that *would* be the greatest loss of his life. He would be living the rest of his days without a heart beating inside his chest.

Sleep had eluded Shaw last night. Thoughts of Lainie, and a future without her and the girls, tormented him. He'd finally taken a hard look at himself and faced his deepest fear. It was more than anxiety about being left again that gripped him. It was fear of not being the man he wanted to be, the man Lainie needed.

Lainie was the whole package. There'd be no easing into married life—if she'd have him. He would be jumping into the deep end of the pool, and he couldn't afford to make a mistake—not with Natalie and Chrissy involved. He had to be sure, because if he failed, he'd risk hurting their little hearts, as well. He knew the pain of a broken marriage and its lasting effects. He could never put those two precious girls through that.

He pulled his truck to a stop in the library parking

lot. He'd been headed for the Filler-up Burger place for lunch. But he'd driven straight to the Dover Library. Apparently, the Lord had a different destination for him. Shaw had prayed last night that he would be worthy of Lainie's love. He was frequently guilty of going his own way, confident in his own direction and forgetting to seek the Lord's direction, only to have the Lord pull him up short and set him straight.

Today, the Father was pointing him toward talking to Lainie and laying his heart at her feet. The outcome was up to the Lord.

The atmosphere in the library was serene and quiet, nothing like the joyful chaos of opening day.

He needed to talk to Lainie, though he had no idea what he'd say. He'd been avoiding her, not wanting to hear about meeting Mrs. Hollingsworth. Petty, but he needed time to accept that Lainie had a new life in front of her, one that didn't include him.

He'd stopped by her back door the night after her mother-in-law had arrived, intending to get some answers. He'd looked into the kitchen and seen them gathered around the table. Her mother-in-law was smiling, the girls were laughing and Lainie looked happier than he'd ever seen her. And he'd never felt so shut out in his life.

Millie looked up and smiled as he approached the main desk. "Hello. What brings you to the library? Something wrong with the woodwork?"

Shaw leaned against the counter, pleased with how well it had turned out. "No. I wanted to talk to Lainie. Is she here?"

"She's not." Millie eyed him closely.

"Do you know where she is?"

"Home probably. Packing."

Shaw's heart stopped. "Packing. Why?"

"Looks like I'll be taking over here, after all. Lainie is going to New Orleans."

He could barely draw breath. She couldn't be leaving. Not after all the work she had put into the library and the way she'd been embraced by the whole town. "Why? She didn't say anything to me."

"I think it just came up. You know her in-laws live there. I guess she felt it was important to have family nearby for the girls."

Shaw didn't even say goodbye. He turned and strode out of the library. He thought he heard a chuckle behind him, but he ignored it. He arrived home and sent up a thankful prayer when he saw Lainie's car. She was still here. He couldn't let her go without telling her how he felt. She might not feel the same way, but he had to try. He would set all his doubts and fears aside.

He walked into her kitchen without knocking. She was standing at the sink and spun around when he entered.

"Shaw? What's wrong? Is everything okay? Is there a problem with the library?"

She was the most beautiful woman he'd ever met, the woman he wanted to spend his life with. The woman he'd risk anything for, including her rejection. "It's fine. Everything is fine. I came to—" He saw the suitcase near the French door he'd installed. It was true. She was leaving. His heart ripped in two.

"Misser Shaw!" Chrissy ran from the living room, her arms held high. He scooped her up and held her close.

"I missed you. I love you, Misser Shaw." She wrapped

her arms around his neck and squeezed, adding a little grunt for good measure.

Shaw's heart felt like it was bursting. "I love you, too, Chrissy." He cradled her head with his palm, wanting this moment to go on forever, wanting to hear her call him Daddy again.

"Hey, Mister Shaw. I'm glad you're home."

Shaw glanced down at the other little charmer. Natalie was smiling up at him like a sunbeam. He set her sister down and held out his arms. "Are you too big to be picked up?"

She shook her head and dashed into his arms. He held her close, too, realizing for the first time how big she was, and how quickly her childhood would pass. He didn't want to miss it.

He looked at Lainie. Her eyes were moist and tinged with concern. He needed to talk to her now. Alone. "Girls, I have something to talk to your mother about. Why don't you go outside and swing. I'll come out soon and push you."

"We have a new grandma, and she has a grandpa, too. We're going to stay with them." Chrissy waved as she hurried out the door.

Lainie searched his face, clearly puzzled by his behavior. He crossed the distance between them, gazing into her warm brown eyes. "Don't go."

"What?"

"Don't leave. I don't want you to go."

"Shaw, it's not—"

He grasped her arms in his hands. "I know you've found a family, but *I* want to be your family. I want to take care of you and the girls. Stay. I'll give you all the time you need."

"What are you saying?"

"I love you. I love those girls. I want to be part of your life and theirs from now on." He reached into his pocket and pulled out the license. "I want this to be real. I want to file it with the court and say the vows and make it legal."

"Shaw, are you sure?"

He saw the doubt in her eyes, the regret. He'd misread so much. She cared for him, but not enough to be his wife. He stepped back, running a hand through his hair. "I'm sure. I've spent most of my life with my heart locked up safe. Too afraid to give it to anyone because they might walk away and leave me alone again. Vicki told me she didn't want to spend her life trying to unlock my heart. I didn't know what she meant then, but I do now. You've unlocked it. You and those little princesses out there."

"You said you didn't want to give up your bachelor life."

"I was a fool. I was afraid to risk a long-term relationship."

"Is this because you feel responsible for us? You think you need to stand in the gap to somehow redeem yourself for the past?"

"No. Yes, I want to be responsible for you and the girls, but only because I want to love and take care of you."

Lainie raised her hands and laid them on his chest, sending his heart racing.

"Are you sure? Because if you're not, you'll break my heart."

Her words took a moment to sink in. He searched

her face, his heart flipping at the love he saw reflected in her brown eyes. She stood on tiptoe and kissed him.

"I think I started falling in love with when you put up the swings for my girls. I've been afraid to tell you."

"Does that mean you'll stay? You won't leave."

"I'm not leaving. I'm just going to New Orleans for the night to meet Mr. Hollingsworth. We'll be back Sunday afternoon."

"But Millie said—" He remembered the chuckle he'd heard on the way out of the library. "Apparently, Millie thought I needed a little incentive to make my move."

"Did you?"

"Yes." He slipped his arms around her waist and hugged her tightly. "I know there's still things from the past between us, but—"

She hushed him with her fingers on his lips. "There's nothing. I said I forgave you, but there was no need. It was an accident. No one's fault. No one to blame. I love you."

"Marry me?"

"You know you're not only asking me, but two other females?"

"Do I need their permission?"

"They already think of you as Daddy."

Shaw chuckled. "Chrissy told me she wanted to buy a new daddy to hug."

Lainie smiled into his eyes, her fingers touching the cleft in his chin. "Then I know what the price of a new daddy should be."

Shaw drew his brows together. "I'm not a rich man, you know."

"I want to keep this house. I want to make it our

home forever, the place we can grow our roots. Together as a family."

"I think I can arrange that. I know a good contractor." He captured her lips, kissing her with all the love he'd locked away, knowing he'd saved it for this moment. This woman. "Should we tell the girls?"

She nodded, slipping her arm around his waist and resting her head on his shoulder. As they passed the table, she picked up the license. "Are you sure this isn't legal?"

"No, but I know where to get one that is. What are you doing Monday morning?"

"Why don't you come to New Orleans with us? I'd like you to meet the Hollingsworths. They're very sweet."

"Won't they be uncomfortable?"

"Irene already suspected I was in love with you, and she encouraged me to be happy and love again."

Arm in arm, they walked across the grass to the swings, where Natalie and Chrissy were being watched over by the faithful Beaux.

"Girls, we have something to tell you." Lainie slipped her arm around his waist. He pulled her close, kissing her forehead.

They smiled at one another. The Lord had brought them together again to heal the past, and find a new future together as a family.

* * * * *

Dear Reader,

I've wanted to give Shaw his own story for a long while now. He first appeared in the second Dover book, Restoring His Heart, as the foreman for the heroine's restoration business. He was a heartbreaker with a soft heart and took a protective stance toward his boss. The next time we see him is in Protecting the Widow's Heart, again as the head of a construction project and casting an appreciative eye toward the heroine. I figured it was time to give the man a woman of his own. So, what better choice than to give the die-hard bachelor a woman with two little girls?

But first both he and the heroine have to deal with forgiveness. Not an easy thing to do for any of us. Even when they confront the past, and forgive, more struggles are waiting.

Sometimes, forgiving someone is merely the door opening to reveal what our real issues are. For Lainie, forgiveness freed her to love again but she fears she's fallen for a man who feels only a sense of responsibility toward her. Shaw finally forgives himself but then must face an even greater fear—the prospect of loving and committing to the woman he loves.

I thoroughly enjoyed writing Lainie and Shaw's story and I hope you'll enjoy spending time with them and in Dover.

I love to hear from readers. You can reach me through Love Inspired Books or at lorrainebeatty.com

Lorraine Beatty

REQUEST YOUR FREE BOOKS!

2 FREE INSPIRATIONAL NOVELS

PLUS 2
FREE
MYSTERY GIFTS

Love Inspired®

YES! Please send me 2 FREE Love Inspired® novels and my 2 FREE mystery gifts (gifts are worth about $10). After receiving them, if I don't wish to receive any more books, I can return the shipping statement marked "cancel." If I don't cancel, I will receive 6 brand-new novels every month and be billed just $4.99 per book in the U.S. or $5.49 per book in Canada. That's a saving of at least 17% off the cover price. It's quite a bargain! Shipping and handling is just 50¢ per book in the U.S. and 75¢ per book in Canada.* I understand that accepting the 2 free books and gifts places me under no obligation to buy anything. I can always return a shipment and cancel at any time. Even if I never buy another book, the two free books and gifts are mine to keep forever.

105/305 IDN GH5P

Name   (PLEASE PRINT)

Address   Apt. #

City   State/Prov.   Zip/Postal Code

Signature (if under 18, a parent or guardian must sign)

Mail to the **Reader Service:**
IN U.S.A.: P.O. Box 1867, Buffalo, NY 14240-1867
IN CANADA: P.O. Box 609, Fort Erie, Ontario L2A 5X3

**Are you a subscriber to Love Inspired® books
and want to receive the larger-print edition?
Call 1-800-873-8635 or visit www.ReaderService.com.**

* Terms and prices subject to change without notice. Prices do not include applicable taxes. Sales tax applicable in N.Y. Canadian residents will be charged applicable taxes. Offer not valid in Quebec. This offer is limited to one order per household. Not valid for current subscribers to Love Inspired books. All orders subject to credit approval. Credit or debit balances in a customer's account(s) may be offset by any other outstanding balance owed by or to the customer. Please allow 4 to 6 weeks for delivery. Offer available while quantities last.

Your Privacy—The Reader Service is committed to protecting your privacy. Our Privacy Policy is available online at www.ReaderService.com or upon request from the Reader Service.

We make a portion of our mailing list available to reputable third parties that offer products we believe may interest you. If you prefer that we not exchange your name with third parties, or if you wish to clarify or modify your communication preferences, please visit us at www.ReaderService.com/consumerchoice or write to us at Reader Service Preference Service, P.O. Box 9062, Buffalo, NY 14240-9062. Include your complete name and address.

LI15

SPECIAL EXCERPT FROM

Love Inspired®

*Can a widow and widower ever leave their grief in the
past and forge a new future—and a family—together?*

*Read on for a sneak preview of
THE AMISH WIDOW'S SECRET.*

"Wait, before you go. I have an important question to ask
you."

Sarah nodded her head and sat back down.

"I stayed up until late last night, thinking about your
situation and mine. I prayed, and *Gott* kept pushing this
thought at me." He took a deep breath. "I wonder, would
you consider becoming my *frau*?"

Sarah held up her hand, as if to stop his words. "I…"

"Before you speak, let me explain." Mose took another
deep breath. "I know you still love Joseph, just as I still
love my Greta. But I have *kinder* who need a mother to
guide and love them. Now that Joseph's gone and the
farm's being sold, you need a place to call home, people
who care about you, a family. We can join forces and help
each other." He saw a panicked expression forming in her
eyes. "It would only be a marriage of convenience. The
girls need a loving mother and you've already proven you
can be that. What do you say, Sarah Nolt? Will you be
my wife?"

Sarah sat silent, her face turned away. She looked into
Mose's eyes. "You'd do this for me? But…you don't
know me."

"I'd do this for us," Mose corrected, and smiled.

The tips of Sarah's fingers nervously pleated and un-pleated a scrap of her skirt. "But we hardly know each other. What would people think? They will say I took advantage of your good nature."

Mose smiled. "So, let them talk. They'd be wrong and we'd know it. I want this marriage for both of us, for the *kinder*. We can't let others decide what is best for our lives. I believe this marriage is *Gott*'s plan for us."

Sarah's face cleared and she seemed to come to a decision. She smoothed out the fabric of her skirt and tidied her hair, then finally took Mose's outstretched hand with a smile. "You're right. This is our life. I accept your proposal, Mose Fisher. I will be your *frau* and your *kinder*'s mother."

Don't miss
THE AMISH WIDOW'S SECRET
by Cheryl Williford,
available June 2015 wherever
Love Inspired® books and ebooks are sold.

Love the Love Inspired book you just read?

Your opinion matters.

Review this book on your favorite book site, review site, blog or your own social media properties and share your opinion with other readers!